THE NEIGHBOR TWO DOORS DOWN

H.K. CHRISTIE

KEEKSTAR MEDIA

Copyright © 2023 by H.K. Christie

Cover design by Odile Stammane

www.authorhkchristie.com

First edition: February 2023

ISBN: 978-1-953268-14-3

211123hc

ONE

FIFTEEN YEARS AGO, I looked like the all-American teen. In my junior year of high school, I had straight As. I was on the cheer squad and played lacrosse. In my free time, if you could call it that, I was captain of the debate team and took part in mock trials. That same year, I took SAT prep classes and studied diligently with a tutor to get the highest possible score on the test. Armed with top grades, numerous extracurriculars, and my dedication to community service — you can't forget the forced selflessness of community service — I visited the top colleges in the United States, knowing I could take my pick. And I hadn't minded all the effort because I enjoyed staying busy and helping others. And I even liked being around my friends and my family. Yes, I was one of those magical teens who actually enjoyed hanging out with my mom, dad, and especially my little sister. She wasn't like a typical annoying younger sister who stole clothes and tried to be everywhere I was. Not that she didn't steal my clothes. She did. I just didn't care, despite the arguments that typically ensued.

She was three years younger, and we were best friends. A

lot of my friends had siblings around the same age and thought they were a nuisance and never let them tag along. That wasn't how it was with Ella and me.

Our parents were happily married, and we lived in a nice house in a nice neighborhood. Mom and Dad told us to spread our wings and follow our passions.

Rare.

That's what we were. And no, I wasn't one of those spoiled teens who did not know how lucky I was. I had volunteered at homeless shelters and handed food out to the unhoused. The universe showed us in vivid color how fortunate we were.

Even after it all fell apart.

In my world, there is a before and an after.

In the after, I tried to stay the same as before. Which we all know is impossible. But that didn't mean I didn't try. I was seventeen and already adept at wearing the right outfit, saying the right things, and acting the right way. Some might say I had prepared for the role my whole life.

At first, they were worried about me. It was obvious in the pity-filled stares from friends, family, and teachers. Maybe they saw the light within me had dimmed, or maybe they were doing what they thought was the right thing. The flowers. The cards. The, "Oh dear, how are you holding up?" question. I had responded with a polite, "It's hard, but we're not giving up."

When really, I wanted to scream, "How the hell do you think I'm doing? I'm shattered!" But that wouldn't be the right thing to say to well-meaning folks.

Within a week, I was back to life like it was before, except now a darkness filled my entire being. But instead of showing it to others, I filled every minute of every day with a distraction. Studying. Sports. Extracurriculars. After I returned to my normal activities and received a near perfect score on my SATs, they stopped being concerned and assumed I was a strong young woman who had handled things so bravely. Or maybe they saw what they wanted to see. Who had time to worry about little old me when there were so many other things to worry about in the world?

After completing my junior year through gritted teeth and silent tears, I sailed right into my senior year, not even taking a break over the summer but choosing to enroll in classes at the local community college. With calculus out of the way senior year, I took on a part-time job while still volunteering at the homeless shelter.

I didn't let my days go blank. That way, my mind couldn't wander to think about before or the dreaded after.

They applauded me for my bravery, my strength, and my resolve to continue to do well in school and to be there for everybody who needed me. When I was accepted into the best colleges in the United States, I was officially what everybody, including myself, wanted me to be.

Following a clear path to excellence was easier than facing the truth that I was nothing without my accomplishments. A shell of a person. I decided on Caltech since it was pretty close to home, and they had a great computer science department. If I hadn't been impressive before, I certainly was when I became one of the few females in the electrical engineering and computer science department at Caltech, one of the top universities for such studies. It was a tough program, and some students didn't thrive under the pressure and competition, but I did. Because I still needed to fill every moment with a distraction from my internal hell.

College was filled with mixers, frat parties, spring break trips to Mexico, and studying. I continued to fool them all with my natural charm and ability to blend in. After graduating with honors, I skipped graduate school to go straight into a lucrative career working at a top tech firm doing computer programming before moving into solutions architecture. Security was most intriguing. I enjoyed finding a system's weak spots and learning how to exploit them.

Maybe I was drawn to this because I worried so much that somebody would dig into me and find my defects. Offense v. Defense? At that point, as a 22-year-old college graduate, nobody had found any. Well, not really. We can often pick out those who are like us. There were a few who saw the real me and befriended me instead of exploiting me. Lucky for me.

Over the years, I was promoted and promoted and promoted again. Did I mention I learned to be exactly the way others wanted me to be? I was perfect for the corporate world. After ten years, I was director of Solutions Architecture at one of the top tech firms in the world.

My façade was flawless.

Until it wasn't.

Although I drowned most of my time at work, I had a few short-term boyfriends. One, two, or three-night stands were more my style. I couldn't let anyone get too close out of fear of them finding the defects inside of me. And I played the role of a successful young woman well. I had my friends from high school. We traveled the world: Paris, London, Barcelona, Brazil, Machu Picchu, and many girls' beach vacays. They all envied me. Nobody stopped to think that maybe it was all an act. That it couldn't go on forever.

Of course, at the time, I didn't know that.

There was no way I could've known. Although maybe if I had talked to someone, a therapist or the grief counselor at the school they offered to everyone after it happened. They could've warned me about what could happen ten, fifteen, or twenty years down the road. For me, I kept up the act for fifteen whole years. And then, bam.

A whole new after.

The after, after.

I wasn't sure how many rounds I'd had, but I remembered the bartender because he was cute, and he kept pouring and giving me that award-winning smile. He mentioned he wanted to be an actor or something like that. I wasn't interested in his career pursuits. What I was interested in was what was underneath that T-shirt and jeans. He flirted, and I flirted back. His come-hither smile was the last thing I remembered before I woke up lying face down on the ground, cuffed, and covered in blood.

There was so much blood. Terror consumed me. It happened so fast. Like a flash. And I couldn't remember. Why was I covered in blood? Why was I being arrested?

The police let me know exactly why they cuffed me once I had calmed down and was restrained to a hospital bed. With a psychiatrist, Dr. Lester, at my bedside, the detective explained I had broken a beer bottle and attacked a man with the broken glass. I slashed at his neck and torso, narrowly avoiding slicing his carotid artery. He was alive but in critical condition.

And that's when I remembered.

Those eyes.

That mouth.

The smirk.

And then it all made sense.

My only regret was that he survived.

It was then, and only then, that I unleashed the rage I had held inside for fifteen years.

With fury, I explained why I had attacked the man. The detective and psychiatrist nodded in fascination as they listened and took notes while I described the events leading up to the attack. The detective assured me he would look into it and try to corroborate the story. I was calm after that. Maybe it was whatever drugs they had pumped me full of or that I finally let it all out. I slept peacefully that night for the first time since the before.

The detective returned to my hospital bed the next day and showed me a photo of the man I had attacked.

My heart nearly stopped.

It wasn't him. But I had been so sure it was. I hadn't attacked the monster that haunted every dream I'd had since that day. I'd almost killed an innocent man. Fear gripped my insides as I wondered what would stop me from doing it again.

TWO

STARING down at the last box, purposefully left for last, I sighed. With the box cutter, I sliced through the packing tape and pulled back the flaps. I picked up the first bubble-wrapped frame and unfastened the tape before unwinding the protective plastic. My heart skipped a beat at the sight of my favorite picture of Ella and me. We were at the beach, our arms around each other with our foreheads pressed together, laughing so hard that we fell to the sand shortly after Dad snapped the photo. It was a good day. I set it atop the fireplace mantle and turned around to take in my new house. It was nice, a quaint two-story craftsman in a suburb of Seattle.

I didn't need all the room, considering all I did at home was work, sleep, and eat, but with the extra rooms, I set up a small gym and a guest room for when Mom visited. It had only taken two days to unpack the entire house after the movers set up the sofas in the living room, the dining table in the kitchen, and my bed and dressers upstairs in my room. The only things I was waiting on were my new treadmill and the bed and linens I'd ordered for the guest room. According to the app on my phone, they should be delivered by Saturday.

Although eager to be settled into my new life, I hadn't wanted to leave Mom after Dad died, but I knew I needed to get out of the Bay Area. Even though my conviction and sentence — assault with a deadly weapon — only landed me six months in a mental health facility plus a year of probation, everybody knew what happened at the bar that night. I lost my hard-earned position at the company and ended up moving back in with my mom and dad when I was forced to sell my house to cover attorney's fees. After my arrest, they gave me the advice to hire the most expensive criminal defense attorney I could afford. Well, they were expensive. Like a house in the Bay Area plus half of my retirement savings expensive. But without my legal team, I would have likely received a felony conviction and spent time in prison and, when released, had a felony on my permanent record likely to deter any future employers. It would have ruined my career and life.

My parents were more than happy to have me back home. They were worried about me, and my therapist thought it was a good idea. So, there I was, an adult woman in her thirties, living at home. I felt like I had reverted to seventeen years old, living in a house so quiet that if you dropped a pin, you'd hear it. One day, out of boredom and curiosity, I proved my theory. I found a pin in my mother's sewing box and dropped it on the hardwood floor and listened as it echoed throughout the house despite everyone being home. That's what it was like in the after.

In the before, it was much noisier. It wasn't unusual for Ella and me, two teenage girls, to be singing, dancing, laughing, or fighting. Mom and Dad joined in when they could.

Now I'm all alone. I think it's for the best.

It had been five years since the incident in the bar, and I had been in therapy ever since. At first, court-mandated and then because it seemed to make Mom and Dad happy and it didn't hurt to talk about things. My therapist, Dr. Baker, is still helping me through the stages of grief and the delayed PTSD. Who knew PTSD could be first seen fifteen years after the trauma? It was rare, and it happened to me. Surprise. Not only that, but apparently, I had been in the angry and depressed stage for so long I didn't realize there was an acceptance stage, but after talking and processing, I finally accepted what had happened. Ella was gone, and she wasn't coming back. I accepted that. At least, that's what I told Dr. Baker. I'm not sure she believes me.

But the guilt. The guilt would always remain, and I didn't think it would ever go away. Forgiveness was another one I couldn't do. I could never forgive the monster. I didn't know his name, so I aptly named him the monster. He was the man in all the nightmares I'd experienced for the last twenty years. I still talked with my therapist three days a week, seeing as I struggled with the acceptance, guilt, and forgiveness aspects of the past. And if I was being honest, it helped to spew my fury at someone. Of course, the drugs muted it, but it was still there, alive and well. But considering I had gone five years without attacking anybody, Dr. Baker must be doing something right.

I placed the rest of the photographs atop my fireplace mantle and smiled at the pictures of Mom and Dad, Ella, and me. And one of a few buddies and me at my college graduation, along with Mom and Dad. In the before times, smiles reached their eyes. In the after times, they still smiled but not as wide. In almost twenty years, you would think the pain would subside. But it hadn't. Dr. Baker said I had to find my new normal. That included taking medication and practicing what she taught me during our sessions. She explained the flashbacks may return but had provided me with tools to cope with them. If I thought I saw the monster again, I was supposed to count to ten backwards to steady myself and bring myself to the present. Well, like I said, it had been five years, and I hadn't tried to kill anybody, so I kept up with the exercises.

I broke down the last of the boxes and put them in the garage with the rest of them. Never having lived outside of California, the change of scenery excited me. And you couldn't beat Seattle. There were the trees. The downtown. The restaurants. The hiking. The rain. *Coffee.* I returned inside, empowered by my unpacked house, and took my first walk in the new neighborhood.

The sky was a light gray but not menacing with angry clouds. Kind of like me. I shut the door behind me and locked the door. I strolled down my driveway and headed down the road. The houses weren't too close together, which was nice. We weren't on top of each other but not exactly remote, either. I passed the first house on the right, and through the windows, I caught a glimpse of a woman, man, dog, and two little boys. A young family. How sweet. I remembered what that was like. Continuing on to the second driveway, I turned toward the house that looked a lot like mine with its dark shingles and green trim and was surprised to see a man about my age, mid-to-late thirties, walking out of the house. He shut the door behind him. Wearing my friendly neighbor persona, I waved and smiled. I still knew how to do all the right things and say all the right things and be all the right ways.

He waved back and headed toward me. He was cute, with short dark hair and light brown eyes, a sexy five o'clock shadow and, of course, the Seattle uniform of tan hiking pants and a navy-blue fleece. I said, "Hi, I'm Allison. I just moved in two doors down and thought I'd introduce myself."

"Hi, I'm Liam, but I don't live here. I was just visiting my aunt and uncle."

Darn it. I wouldn't mind a hunky neighbor. "Oh, well, if

you ever come around again, you know someone two doors down," I said in a friendly tone like a friendly person would say it, but slightly embarrassed.

"New in town?" he asked with a slight grin.

"How can you tell?"

"Well, for starters, you're wearing a T-shirt and a pair of leggings. It's likely to rain any minute."

"Guilty. I just moved here from the Bay Area."

He nodded. "That explains it. Here in Seattle, it can rain at any moment. You always need to have a fleece or a raincoat handy."

"Good to know. I'll add those to my list."

"What brings you to Seattle?"

"A job. I start at Troodle Tech on Monday."

Recognition sparkled in his eyes. "I work at Troodle."

"What department are you in?"

"I'm in software applications. You?"

"IT - Finance."

"No kidding? You must be Allison Smythe. You're the new director of IT - Finance, right?"

"Guilty, again," I said with a smile.

"I saw your resume. Quite impressive."

He had already checked me out? I was feeling disadvantaged. "How long have you been at Troodle Tech?"

"Just a few months. I'm also a transplant. Southern California. This is my first time living outside of California. It's been quite a change, but it's nice. It grows on you."

"My first time, too."

"Well, welcome. I have to jet, but maybe I'll see you on Monday. Good luck on your first day."

"Thanks."

Not too shabby. A cute boy. A new job. It wasn't completely surprising that the first person I talked to in the neighborhood worked at Troodle, considering it was the largest employer in the Seattle area. He waved as he climbed into his car. Despite his warnings about the rain, I watched his Subaru Forrester drive off before continuing down the road. Sure enough, just moments later, I felt drops on the top of my head and prickling on my arms. I certainly wasn't in California anymore.

THREE

My cheeks were tired from smiling all day. The number of times I said, "It's so great to meet you. I look forward to working together," it would have been more efficient to record the greeting and play it whenever I came across a new coworker. Everybody seemed enchanted by my warm and friendly demeanor. It was the persona I had been building since my teen years. Just because I now saw a therapist and took medication for my anxiety and depression didn't mean I couldn't still fake it until I made it. Even when I had made it, I still faked it.

Maybe that wasn't true. I wasn't a bad person and was warm and friendly with people I cared about. Plus, I was a manager and had to set an example. My promotion of teamwork and initiative with a pleasant working attitude would be a guide for how my employees should interact with one another and with me. It was funny to think that someone who had nearly murdered another person was the manager of five engineers. If they only knew.

But if I had learned nothing else in my years of corporate service, it wasn't always the smartest person who got all the promotions and the money; it was the person who had passable skills and the ability to work with others. IQ and EQ were equally important. IQ was a measure of a person's ability to use logic and grasp complex ideas, which was certainly important in engineering, whereas EQ determined a person's ability to recognize emotion in oneself and others, using that awareness to guide decisions. For example, your boss learned two minutes ago his wife died. Someone with a decent EQ knows it's not a good time to complain that the guy in the cubicle next to you chews his food too loud. If I could give any new employee advice, it would be, "Do your job and don't be a jerk." It really isn't that difficult — yet, so many find it to be unsurmountable. Sigh.

After having one-on-one meetings with my new reports, it disappointed me to learn not all were adequate in the EQ department. There is always at least one. Marvin. The rest of the bunch were pretty solid. Marvin, on the other hand, seemed to think his phone was more important than the meeting with his new boss. Would he be so glued to his phone when he should've been engaging with me and the rest of the team if he knew what I was capable of?

Not that I would tell them.

Thankfully, my misdemeanor conviction meant that I could still hold a job. I was not label a felon like I could've been. And because I was such a stellar employee before the incident, I received a glowing recommendation from my old job, even though they didn't want me back. Even with all my tragedies, I was still lucky. Why didn't I feel it? I shook my head. I wasn't supposed to have those types of thoughts. Dr. Baker said I deserved my success and to be happy and healthy.

Sitting in my new office, I stared out the window and thought, "This truly is the beginning of the rest of my life." And

I was going to take every opportunity I could to get past what I had done, not only to the man in the bar but to Ella, too.

It was my fault he took her.

It was a week after my seventeenth birthday, and I thought I was hot stuff driving around in my new baby-blue Honda Civic that Mom and Dad surprised me with. I loved that car and so did Ella, who rode shotgun every chance she got. It had been a sunny Saturday afternoon when I said to Ella, "Hey, you want to go get ice cream?"

She had nodded her head wildly, her strawberry blonde hair whipping around. "Ice cream! Ice cream!"

Shaking my head, I said, "Okay, weirdo. You're not coming with me if you plan to act like a lunatic."

She brushed her hair out of her face. "Yes, madam. I'd love to join you for an outing. I'm quite proper now," she said with a fake British accent.

We had erupted into a fit of giggles, and I grabbed my keys before running out to the driveway. Ella was the silly, creative one. The yin to my yang.

In my car, I started the engine and blasted the stereo. As we drove down the road, we sang along to Pink's *Let's Get This Party Started* until we reached the grocery store downtown. Parked, we belted out the last lyric before turning off the car. I glanced toward the front of the store and spotted Josh. I had the biggest crush on him since the beginning of the school year. He hadn't asked me out yet, but we danced at prom, so I knew he liked me at least a little. I turned to Ella. "Stay here for a sec, okay? I want to go *bump* into Josh."

Ella nodded. "Cool."

I jumped out of the car and ran across the parking lot and then slowed to a casual stroll, as if I didn't have a care in the world. Josh spotted me and our eyes met. "Oh, hi, Josh. How are you?"

He smirked like the cocky teen boy he was. "Cool. Just picking up some snacks for the team. What are you up to?"

"Just picking up some ice cream."

"Cool. Well, I gotta jam."

I turned around to wave for Ella to join me, but when I did, she wasn't in the car. Ella was struggling with a man. I sprinted toward her as she screamed, and the man grabbed her legs and threw her into a van. His eyes locked with mine before he disappeared, and the van sped off. I fell to my knees and screamed. Josh ran over, and while I was hysterically trying to explain Ella had been taken, he dialed 9-1-1.

It was the last time I ever saw Ella.

If I hadn't wanted to fake-casually bump into Josh, Ella would've been with me inside the grocery store buying ice cream. Instead, she had been abducted by some creepy man, a monster with dark hair, dark eyes, and a pointed chin.

I gave the description to the police, but it was of no use. The van didn't have any license plates, and my description was too generic. Nobody ever offered any credible tips, but the police received a handful of fake tips from crackpots, making our lives even worse than they already were.

It was my fault she was taken.

In a few weeks, Ella will have been missing twenty years.

That's the guilt. No amount of drugs or therapy or talking or moving could make that guilt go away. Dr. Baker said it was possible he could have taken both of us if I was with her, or he could've waited until we came out of the store to take her. She says that I had no role in Ella's disappearance, but I didn't believe that. I was guilty. Lock me up.

The knock on the door brought me back to the present day. "May I come in?"

"Of course."

Liam sat down in the chair in front of my desk. "Nice digs."

"I like it," I said with a smile, a smile that may be permanently affixed to my face if I didn't get out of that office soon.

"How was your first day?"

I gave my standard response. "It was great. It was nice to meet the team, and I had lunch with the VPs and senior directors. They all seem like a really great bunch of people to work with."

"I hear good things about your team. Are you done for the day?"

"I'm just waiting for IT to finish configuring my phone." A company phone, the perfect way of making the worker bees available to the company twenty-four-hours a day.

"Well, that could be a while. I'd love to treat you to a cupcake."

"A cupcake?" That was an original pick-up line.

"There's a new bakery right around the corner. Fantastic cupcakes. My treat. By the time we're done, your phone will be ready."

A cute guy and a cupcake? Yes, please.

FOUR

Sweets were one of the few vices I had left since I was supposed to avoid booze. Considering alcohol didn't mix well with my medication, and of course, there's that whole I might murder somebody if I got too drunk thing. That night at the bar was the last time I'd tasted the sweet, sweet burn of alcohol.

The bakery was one of those ridiculously pink and floral spots. The proprietor must have had a sugar induced dream, and it turned into this. It was cute and filled with pastel pastries, thick sandwiches, and bright salads to go. Liam told me to pick a table while he ordered for us, claiming he knew the owner and had the inside scoop into the best flavors of the day. Seated at a small table for two, I stared out the large windows at the folks who wore business suits and serious expressions walking past. A few minutes later, Liam joined me. "So, who do you want the dirt on?"

"The dirt?"

"On your team. I can tell you where some of the bodies are buried."

Interesting choice of words. But hey, if he had intel, I

wanted it. "My team includes Jarvis, Karen, Dave, Dusty, and Marvin. I can say that after our meeting today, four of them seem like good eggs. One of them, I may have a few concerns about."

Liam smirked. "Marvin."

"Bingo."

"Marvin is smart, but he rubs people the wrong way. As you may have noticed. Not only that, but word around the office cooler is he applied for your job and obviously didn't get hired, and now you're his boss — a woman ten years younger. You're what, twenty-nine?"

With that, I laughed out loud. He was a clever one. "Thirty-seven. You?"

"Thirty-eight."

He was of an appropriate age. "Any other office dirt I need to know?"

"There's a few you may not want to shake hands with because they don't wash them after they use the bathroom. I'll give you a list."

Yuck. "What about the higher ups? Anyone to avoid?"

"Rumor is your group is pretty solid. You're lucky you landed here when you did. There's a lot of exciting things going on at Troodle and with your team, so you're golden. Just maybe give Marvin some time. He's pretty bitter about you getting the job over him."

"Noted."

A woman in her fifties with dark hair and bright green eyes said, "For Liam and his friend, I have a lemon chiffon and a red velvet," before setting them down on the table.

"Thanks, Cora."

He knew the server by name?

He said, "This is Allison. She's the one I was telling you about. She moved into the house two doors down from you."

Oh, it was his aunt. I was already meeting his family? And my neighbor.

Cora said, "Oh, well then, welcome to the neighborhood, Allison. It's good to meet you. Where are you from?"

"California. The Bay Area."

Cora looked stricken but then said, "Oh, it's lovely there. It's been years since I've been. Again, welcome," before rushing off.

"She seems nice. Are you close?"

"No, not really. Before I moved up here, I hadn't seen her since I was a kid. This weekend, I met her daughter, my cousin, for the first time, and she's fourteen."

Cora returned with two white porcelain cups filled with espresso. "Two espressos."

"Sugar and caffeine are my favorite combination," I said, trying to be friendly.

"Mine too."

"Liam says you have a daughter. Does she work here, too?" I asked, knowing people love it when you asked about their children.

Cora shook her head. "No, she's at home enjoying her summer."

"Maybe you should have her work here over the summer. Keep her busy and teach her some responsibility," Liam suggested.

Cora nodded. "Now that's an interesting idea."

A customer walked into the store. "It was great to meet you, Allison. Enjoy the cupcake."

We waved. What a nice person. Was it genuine, or did she wear a mask like I did? I picked up the fork and stabbed into the red velvet cupcake topped with cream cheese frosting and red heart sprinkles on top. I shoved it in my mouth with the grace of a garbage truck driver before I shut my eyes and moaned slightly. It was heaven.

"That good, huh?"

I had nearly forgotten I wasn't alone. I glanced at Liam. "It's pretty good. I'll have a dozen more, please."

"That could be arranged. Do you want to try my lemon chiffon?"

"Yes, I would."

He put a forkful on his utensil and handed it to me. The lemon chiffon was tangy and sweet, even better than the red velvet. Liam fidgeted. "So... do you have a boyfriend? Girlfriend? Kids?"

A rap sheet? He was fishing to know about my personal life. Definitely a romantic prospect — perhaps a fun weekend filled with cupcakes and Liam. "No boyfriend, no kids, just me. You?" So far, I was enjoying this first... whatever this was.

"Single, no kids, and never been married. So, if you have time this weekend, I could show you around Seattle."

He had game, I'd give him that.

With a knowing glance, I said, "I'd like that." I glanced at my watch and said, "I better hurry and get my phone. Thanks for the cupcake. It was amazing."

"You're very welcome."

On the way back to the office, we flirted, and I was certain I had a crush. For the first time in a long time, I felt hopeful that life could be better and not only filled with darkness. It was that, or I was all hopped up on sugar and caffeine.

He escorted me to my office, where a man stood near the door holding a smart phone. Liam said, "I'll see you later."

I nodded before turning my attention to the man. "Edgar?" Edgar was the man I spoke with from the IT helpdesk.

He nodded and handed my phone to me. "You're all set. Email and the shared drives will update automatically, and I've installed all the applications you may need so that you can work from your phone basically anytime, anywhere."

That's what companies do to enable you to work for them twenty-four hours a day, seven days a week, anywhere in the world. You've got to love a giant corporation filled with smarties. "Now, I can work any time I'm breathing."

"This isn't your first rodeo."

I scrolled through the screens and recognized the work-related apps. All pretty standard in the biz. "Certainly not. You have a good night."

"You too, and welcome to Troodle." With that, Edgar waved and exited my office.

I picked up my shiny-new laptop and power supply and slipped them into my new Troodle Tech branded backpack that matched my new Troodle Tech zip-up fleece, ball cap, and travel mug. Everything about my day was so brutally normal. It was wonderful. I really couldn't ask for any more, could I? Not to mention I had a date this weekend with a hunky guy who was smart, funny, and had a serious cupcake hook up.

Maybe pick up a salad or sandwich for dinner tonight? It would save me the trouble of boiling water for a pasta dinner. Backpack on, I took the stairs down — because it was Seattle, and in Seattle, you take the stairs — and exited the building to head back to the bakery to pick up that salad and sandwich for dinner. Maybe another cupcake. I hadn't walked ten steps outside of the lobby when I saw him.

That hair, now salt and pepper.

Those eyes, now with fine lines at the corners.

He was twenty years older.

But it was him.

It was the monster.

My heart pounded and my head swirled. I stepped back, pressed my face up against the cement building, slipped off my beaded bracelet, and began counting the colorful orbs. One. Two. Three. Four. Five. Six. Seven. Eight. Nine. Ten. Eleven. Twelve. After a few deep breaths, I inched forward and peeked around the corner again. There were dozens of people on the streets in all directions, but he was gone. The monster was gone.

It couldn't be him. It had to be a flashback. A hallucination. I was sober.

Maybe the day had been more stressful than I thought and it triggered the hallucination. I hurried back into the building and went down to the parking garage to my car.

Safely inside, I pulled out my cell phone. As it rang, I contemplated what this meant. Was I losing my mind? Could I not control the hallucinations? The flashbacks. I had counted the beads. I had taken deep breaths and didn't attack anybody.

Finally, she answered. "Hello."

"Dr. Baker, it's Allison Smythe."

"What's wrong, Allison?"

As quick as I could, I said, "I saw him. I thought I saw him."

"Slow down. Tell me from the beginning exactly what happened."

I explained my first day of work, even the trip to the bakery with Liam all the way through, receiving my configured phone and walking down the street and seeing the monster. The man with the dark hair, the dark eyes, and the pointed chin. And how I had done my exercises, and then he was gone.

"This could be a reaction to your first day at work and the move to a new city. You probably have nothing to worry about, but just in case, we can start a daily check-in if you think that would help? There have been a lot of changes for you this week. Plus the upcoming anniversary. It's not surprising that it has triggered your symptoms."

Symptoms triggered. Symptoms like seeing the monster?

Symptoms like I might attack another innocent man. Hyperventilating, I heaved as Dr. Baker said, "Allison, listen to me. Just breathe and count your beads. You'll be okay. You'll get through this."

I started counting my beads again.

"Where are you right now?"

"I'm in my car in the parking garage at work."

"Do you feel calm enough to drive home?"

Was I calm? Was I seeing monsters? In daylight, while sober? I had always assumed the alcohol had contributed to that night in the bar, but if I was seeing things sober, what did that mean? "Yes."

"When you get home, maybe make yourself some herbal tea and have dinner. Do you have healthy food in the house?"

"I have stuff for pasta and peanut butter sandwiches." Mom had packed some staples for me, insisting I take it with me because moves were tiring, and I may not want to rush out to the grocery store if I were hungry. She was right.

"After you have some dinner and tea, you can call me if you need to, okay?"

She was speaking to me like I was a child. I really hated that. "Thank you."

"Drive safe. I'll talk to you soon."

Feeling slightly more centered, I drove out of the parking garage and headed home. The sky seemed brighter, and there were more people out than I remembered. I needed to get home, eat, and reduce my stimuli. But on the way, I couldn't help but wonder if I was losing my mind. Would things get worse? What was next? Would I see the bogeyman and the Loch Ness monster too? How long would this go on?

FIVE

CORA

WITH ONE ARM wrapped around a paper bag full of day-old pastries, I pull out my key to unlock the front door to our home. First the bottom lock and then the deadbolt. Both locks were always engaged, when we were inside or outside. It was a rule, and I learned over the years to not break the rules. Not if I wanted to avoid the consequences. I pushed the door open, scooted inside, and shut the door behind me. Still balancing the bag, I relocked the bottom and deadbolt. Secure, I walked into our home.

It was beautiful. Immaculate. The way Edison wanted it. More accurately, the way he demanded it. Even when Ruby came along, things still had to remain spotless, even with the baby, a toddler, a child, a preteen, and now a teen. I stepped into our kitchen with its white cabinets and marble countertops and shiny chrome appliances and called out, "I have cupcakes."

Ruby ran into the kitchen. "What flavors did you bring home?"

"Your favorite, red velvet."

"Can I have one now? Before Dad gets home."

Ruby was a sharp girl and had taken to the rules like they were gospel. But to be fair, she didn't really know any other way. "Have you heard from your father?"

"Not yet."

"Well then, we should probably wait until after dinner. Okay?"

Ruby's face fell. I hated disappointing her. But she knew the rules. Edison was quite clear about the fact that gluttony was a punishable offense. He used to weigh me every week. He had let up over the last few years, though. I wasn't sure why, but I certainly didn't question it. Not that I didn't stay trim and exercise every day.

"What's for dinner?"

"I'm going to heat the lasagna that I made yesterday. How does that sound?"

"Can I help make the salad?"

"That would be great."

I lifted the cupcakes out of the paper bag and set them on the counter. Despite Edison's rules regarding our waistlines, he had a bit of a sweet tooth, too. It was one thing that brought us together all those years ago.

Glancing back at Ruby as she rummaged through the refrigerator for the salad fixings, I thought about what a lovely young woman she was becoming. She was fourteen years old and had seen little of the world outside of our home and neighborhood, and I regretted that. It wasn't fair, but it was how he wanted things. I shouldn't really complain or think badly of him. At this point, I tried to forget the past and live in the present. Considering he had let me open the bakery three months ago, I was grateful. I couldn't believe it when he'd agreed and said that I was one of the best bakers he knew and it would be a shame to not share my gift with the rest of the world. I almost fainted from the shock. He had kept us under a strict regime for so long, any kindness was shocking. But again, I didn't question it.

Edison hadn't let me work outside of the house since we were married thirty-five years ago. Owning my business and working at the bakery allowed me to meet new people, even if for a few moments, to ask them about their favorite cake flavors, or cookie varieties, or suggestions for the next sandwiches and salads to be added to the menu. If his willingness to loosen the reins on me hadn't been baffling enough, he had finally agreed to let Ruby go to public school after being homeschooled her whole life. She would start high school in the fall. Ruby practically did cartwheels when she heard the news. Even though Ruby's social interactions had been limited, I knew she was a people person and would thrive in the real world. She knew little about the world, and teenagers could be downright evil.

But despite my worries, I believed she'd excel in school and make tons of friends. She wasn't like your typical teen. She was helpful around the house, without being asked, and kept a sunny disposition even when Edison was in one of his moods. But maybe all that would change when she met other people her own age, and she would turn into one of those awful teenagers that I read about. I couldn't even imagine it. But then again, she was her father's daughter.

As Ruby chopped a tomato, I said, "I was talking to our new neighbor and Liam at the shop today. Liam had an interesting idea. He suggested maybe you could work at the bakery this summer before you start school in the fall. I could use the extra help."

Ruby stopped chopping and her mouth dropped open. "Are you serious? You would let me have a job at the bakery?"

"I will have to talk to your father to make sure it's okay with him, but yes. I'd love to have you there. If you want to."

Her eyes sparkled. "Yes! Oh, my gosh. Yes!"

She was a beautiful young woman with her strawberry blonde hair and dazzling blue eyes and full lips. So full of life. She should be out there taking the world by storm. "I'll ask your dad tonight. You'll have to help me convince him."

"Of course!" She wrapped her arms around me, hugged tight, and whispered, "Thank you so much, Mom."

Now I only hoped that Edison would agree to the summer job. The sound of the front door opening made my body rigid, and I stepped away from Ruby. He was home. He'd been in a pretty good mood lately, but being on edge when he was near was part of my muscle memory. You never knew what kind of mood he'd be in when he came home. He walked into the kitchen with a smile. "My two girls."

My body relaxed. Ruby ran over to him and wrapped her arms around his middle. "Hi, Daddy."

He kissed the top of her head. "Ruby, how was your day?"

"It was pretty good. I was helping make a salad to go with the lasagna for dinner." Ruby eyed me.

I said, "We were just discussing the idea of her picking up some hours at the bakery. Only if you think it's a good idea, of course."

He looked down at Ruby's pleading eyes and back at me. "I'll allow it under a few conditions."

Of course, there were conditions. There were always conditions. There was a rule for just about everything we did in our lives. He said it taught us discipline and kept things in order. Except we weren't periodicals on a shelf. We were human beings. But he didn't really care about that.

"First, Ruby can only go to the bakery. No wandering off into the city by yourself, okay?"

Ruby nodded enthusiastically.

"Second, I want your work schedule posted at home, so I

know where you are and when you'll be home and when you'll be at the bakery. Okay?"

She did another enthusiastic nod.

"Last, I'll drive you there and take you home."

"Thank you, Daddy!" She squeezed him harder.

He patted her on the back of the head like a dog. Ruby's affection for her father was undeniable. Probably because she didn't know him like I did. She had no idea who he really was.

He smiled like he was God. "It will be a good work experience for you. What a great idea, Cora."

A compliment. Thank goodness I had nothing in my mouth, or I would've choked.

Ruby unwrapped herself from her father and went back over and began slicing the lettuce. I said, "I met our new neighbor who moved in two houses down. Liam brought her into the bakery."

"Who is this new neighbor? How did you know she was our neighbor?"

I'll get to it. Jeez. "Liam brought her in. They work together, and they got to talking, and turns out she lives two houses down. She seems really nice, and I think Liam is quite smitten with her."

"You didn't invite her over here, did you? You remember the rules, don't you?"

How could I forget? No outsiders without express permission from Edison. We were not allowed to leave the house or make social arrangements or practically do anything without Edison's stamp of approval. "I didn't invite her over."

"Good. I'm going to take a shower. Dinner will be ready when I'm done."

I smiled. "Of course." I could choose to believe it was a question, but I knew it was a command. *Whatever. Go shower off the scent of your girlfriend.* I didn't care. Yes, my husband was having an affair. Obviously, I had been suspicious when he'd become more lenient with me and Ruby, like allowing me to open a bakery, funded with his salary, and allowing Ruby to attend public school. Not to mention he hadn't requested sex from me in almost three years. I knew something had preoccupied him, and one day, when I was doing the laundry, I found some interesting receipts in his pockets. A hotel in the middle of the day. A restaurant downtown. He was definitely sleeping with someone. All I could think was *better her than me.*

SIX

I HAD MADE it to the weekend without another sighting of the monster, which I was thankful for. Daily meetings with my therapist were annoying but necessary. She helped me stay grounded in reality. It seemed so real. But Dr. Baker explained, it may not be the last time I have a flashback.

But if it was a flashback, how had he aged?

Dr. Baker said it could be a hallucination or my mind playing tricks. It was unsettling to not be able to trust my mind when I'd spent most of my life using it to get me everything I wanted, but now it was failing me. Questioning what was reality and what wasn't was rough.

Thankfully, I'd made it through my first week at work without incident. Still had a job. Check. I credited that with the daily check-ins with Dr. Baker, which helped me maintain my façade of being a woman who was completely together and in control of her life.

It had been five years since I had a flashback or thought I'd seen the monster. Why now? Dr. Baker assured me it was likely the stress of the move and new job, both big life events that I had coupled together. She'd warned me about going out with Liam, but between you and me, seeing him was the only thing I was looking forward to. He looked like he could be one great stress reliever. If you know what I mean. But maybe it was more than that with him. Something about his smile, his eyes, made me want to get to know him better. Which was terrifying. If I learned more about him, surely he would want to learn more about me. What would he think if he knew the truth?

Despite my high achiever status throughout my adult life, I never had a relationship that lasted more than a month or two. I didn't know what was wrong with me. That's not true. Clinical depression and post-traumatic stress disorder. That was the clinical diagnosis, anyway. Dr. Baker said maybe it was too much too soon to go on a date with Liam. A date that was likely a date and not a precursor to casual sex, like most of my dates turned out to be. Not that men hadn't wanted a second, third, or tenth date. I didn't want to go there. Dr. Baker thought it was a way of punishing myself, by not allowing myself to have the things I had wanted in life, like a husband and children of my own. Now, at thirty-seven years old, the odds I would have a family of my own were slipping away faster than a snake on a plane. It was for the best. I obviously couldn't be trusted to keep a child safe after allowing my sister to be stolen by a monster.

Maybe I should cancel with Liam. He seemed like one of those wholesome guys who wanted a white-picket fence and two children, a boy and a girl. One of each! Ick. I should cancel.

Or maybe I was overthinking it. As soon as he learned what I had done — first I let my sister get kidnapped and then I tried to kill a man, an innocent man I'd never met before — he'd surely run for the hills. I took a sip of my peppermint tea and stared at the cupcakes on my countertop. Liam was sweet. Maybe that's what was different. And I worked with him. If it ended badly, it would be awkward at work and could jeopardize my position. I should cancel.

My phone buzzed. A text from Liam, asking if I liked sushi. Of course, *I love sushi*. Almost as much as cupcakes and coffee. Well, I had to give Liam credit. He was obviously on to the fact that he could win me over with good food and coffee. I picked up the phone and set down my tea. I texted back.

Love it

Perfect. See you at 3

I shook my head as I contemplated a reply. Why was this so hard? I was being ridiculous. This wasn't that big of a deal. I texted back.

CU @3

He told me he wanted to take me down to Pike Place and roam around Pioneer Square. Followed by a stroll along the water and taking a peek at some local art exhibits. And sampling the tastes of Seattle. Sounded great. I just hoped one or both of us didn't get hurt.

A KNOCK on my door set off the butterflies. I grabbed my crossbody bag and headed toward the front door. Before I opened it, I peeked through the peephole and there he stood, casual and carefree. I opened the door and couldn't suppress the smile creeping onto my face. "You brought me flowers?"

"Of course. This is a date, right?"

I nodded my head. "Yeah, it's a date." In all my years, I didn't think I ever had a date bring me flowers. Maybe prom? It was sweet, albeit a little silly considering we were in Seattle and surrounded by greenery. But the flowers were pretty, and I'd read an article saying they reduce your cortisol levels, so they were exactly what I needed. Less stress meant fewer flashbacks and less murdering innocent strangers.

"So, this is your place?"

Realizing I hadn't invited him in, I said, "Yep. Come on in, and I'll show you around."

He wiped his feet on the mat and entered. "Looks like you're all unpacked already."

"All it took was a little project management, and I had all of my stuff delivered and unpacked over the weekend."

He walked over to the fireplace. My heart rate sped up. Would he ask about my family? About Ella?

He squinted and said, "Who is this with you?"

"That's my sister, Ella. It was taken quite a few years ago." I chuckled, trying to make light of the situation that the girl in the photo was kidnapped just a week later.

He seemed disturbed, but smiled and said, "Are you close?"

We were. Did I tell him the truth? Dr. Baker told me acceptance was my next step, and I was almost there. Fake it till I made it. "She died."

"I'm so sorry."

He looked back at the photo again and cocked his head.

"What is it?" I asked.

"Oh, nothing. She looks familiar, is all."

Had he seen her photos on the news all those years ago? And then on each anniversary of her disappearance over the next ten years? "She was kidnapped almost twenty years ago. It was all over the news. You might've seen it."

He stared at the photo again and said, "That must be it." Without taking his eyes off the picture, he cleared his throat. "That must have been difficult for you. How old were you?"

"I had just turned seventeen."

"I'm so sorry."

There it was. The pity. Ick. I hated it. I shrugged. "Thanks."

"They found her?"

Shaking my head, I said, "No."

"Oh, I just thought... you said she died."

My spine stiffened. "We assume. It's been almost twenty years."

"Oh."

Did he look pale? Had I already ruined our date? Maybe I should have cancelled. I should have known he'd see the photos and ask questions. Avoidance. It had worked for twenty years. "Do you want to see the rest of the house?"

He seemed uneasy. "Sure."

The vibe in the room had definitely shifted. Was he weirded out that my sister was kidnapped and now probably dead? Not probably. She was dead. She was gone, and she wasn't coming back. That was what I was supposed to tell myself.

As I gave him the grand tour of my three bedroom, two bath home, he acted interested and impressed. Maybe he was good at avoidance, too? Or maybe he was just being polite.

When we reached the sliders to the back yard, I said, "And this is the best part." I flipped the latch and slid open the door and stepped onto the deck. "This is why I bought this house."

My back yard was like a forest of trees and distant mountain views. There was something about it I couldn't resist. When I saw it on the video, I told my realtor to make an offer.

The sparkle returned to his eyes. "Very nice."

The only furniture I hadn't ordered was patio furniture and a barbecue. Maybe I'd get a fire pit, too. That would be nice in the cool months. Sipping on tea wrapped in a blanket or the warm arms of a hunky man, like Liam. Assuming he didn't run screaming after our date. "Shall we get going?"

"Yes, you're going to love downtown. And the sushi — it melts in your mouth."

"I can't wait."

With that, we reentered the house. I locked the slider and headed toward the door. I grabbed the handle and was about to step outside when I saw Liam stop in front of the living room and fixate on the photo once more. His brow furrowed. He looked at me and gave me a pathetic fake grin and approached. "Okay, let's go."

"After you."

I watched him walk toward his car with his head bowed, and something about his energy caused an uneasy feeling to creep inside of me. Shaking my head, I thought, *No. He is normal, and this momentarily depressing vibe will pass.*

SEVEN

WELL, it was going great until it wasn't. After the weird vibes in the house, I had finally lightened the mood as we strolled Pike Place, sampling cookies, freshly baked bread, and coffee. I thought maybe I had imagined the uneasiness coming off Liam before and that maybe it was all from the part of my brain that sometimes saw people who weren't really there.

Nope.

At dinner, I had just taken a bite of salmon nigiri, enjoying the buttery texture and freshness of the rice dunked in a perfect mix of wasabi and soy sauce, when it fell apart. It started with a question about my last job. After a cheery explanation that I had worked from home the last few years, wanting to be close to my mom and dad, knowing that Dad was sick and I didn't want Mom to be all alone, Liam had said, "I can't believe you left Block — talk about a dream job."

"It was great. I was there for ten years, but then I needed some time off."

"How come?"

I could tell he didn't buy the generic reasoning for why I

had left one of the world's most premier social media companies, working in their security department and quickly rising
through the ranks. It made little sense unless something tragic
had happened, like I killed someone or had tried to. "I was
going through some personal things and took a break."

"A break?"

Why wasn't he letting it go? My gut was telling me he
already knew the entire story, and he was just checking to see if
I was a liar or crazy or both. "I was having some stress issues,
and the doctors felt it was important for me to get rest and
treatment."

Would that be enough to get him to move on from what I
obviously didn't want to talk about? Nope.

"It's just that when Troodle was vetting you, I reached out
to a friend at Block and asked what your story was."

There it was. He was asking me my story when he had
already asked somebody else. Who does that? Was this all some
sort of sick game for him, making me pretend like he was interested when really all he wanted was the scoop on Block's top
security architect who had a psychotic break and almost killed
a stranger?

My heart was racing, and I was wondering if I should ditch
him and get a ride share back to my house. I was not interested
in whatever little game he was playing. "Look, it was a difficult
time. I don't enjoy talking about it, okay? And if you already
know the story, then why are you asking me?"

At that point, I figured the date was pretty much toast. He
shook his head. "I'm sorry. I didn't mean to upset you. My
friend just made it seem like your departure was a little sudden.
We can change the subject. How's the maguro?"

I set down my chopsticks. Perhaps I jumped the gun a bit.
Maybe he really was just wondering if he was going on a date
with a psycho. Or if his aunt and uncle now lived two doors

down from a psycho. Dr. Baker insisted I was not a psycho and that having PTSD was very different. Plus, I had no incidents — not really — in the last five years.

Surrendering to the moment, I told him everything about what happened at the bar, my time at the mental health facility, and being on probation. He seemed more interested than horrified, which was a plus. But then he asked what I was most afraid he'd ask. "Nothing like that happened to you again?"

I figured there would be no second date, so what the hell? I could get another job and sell the house and run away. "Well, my therapist and I talk three times a week, and sometimes more. She explained to me that stress can trigger the flashbacks, so I might think I see the monster, but it's not really him. And with the stress of the move and the new job, she thinks it could cause symptoms, but it's nothing to be concerned about. I don't really drink anymore, not really at all. I've replaced most of my alcohol consumption with herbal tea and black coffee. As you can tell, I love excellent coffee and baked goods. I think you're on to me there." Was I rambling? Did he think I was cute or deranged? I swear I couldn't tell anymore.

"So, you're okay? You're not going to freak out and stab me?" he asked with a playful smirk.

I hoped it was playful.

"It's not likely. I mean, you don't even look like him. And you're too young. He's probably fifty now. Unless you are, in fact, fifty and have aged extremely well," I added, trying to lighten the horribly dark mood.

"No, I'm still thirty-eight, and I'm glad to hear that you will not stab me. Now, that maguro may want to be worried." He chuckled.

Did he really not care about my past? Or at least not think I was a freak? Maybe it was best that he knew all the gory details.

I sat silently, not sure what to say.

He cleared his throat. "I'm sorry I brought up all that stuff. But I'm glad you told me. I like you and hope I haven't scared you off with all my questions."

My lips parted to speak, but I found myself speechless again. He was still interested in me after all of that? How was that even possible? "No worries. And no, you haven't scared me off." *Well, at least I have something new to talk about in therapy.*

The server brought a rainbow roll and set it down between Liam and me. Liam said, "This is my favorite. This way, you get to taste all their best sushi and fresh crab."

Reclaiming my chopsticks, I popped a piece into my mouth and savored the flavors. "You're right, it does not disappoint."

I thought after a few bumps, *This date has really turned around.* Ha.

After sushi, we strolled through Pioneer Square and stopped in at the Elliott Bay Book Company, a massive, multi-level, independent bookstore. As we browsed the stacks, I learned Liam was an avid reader and loved all things Agatha Christie and other detective mysteries.

The skies darkened, and so we headed back. Feeling lighter as we headed for Liam's car, my heart fluttered when he reached out to hold my hand. In that second, I thought, *Wow, this turned out to be the best day I've experienced in I don't know how long.* His hand was warm and comfortable. We turned to gaze into each other's eyes, and he gave me a kind smile. He had to be some kind of saint or something. I said, "I had fun today."

"Me too. I certainly hope we can do this again."

I nodded in agreement.

We reached Liam's SUV, and he opened the door for me like a 1950s gentleman. It was unnecessary but nice. I climbed in and looked over my shoulder before turning back toward the door to shut it when my heart beat in my ears and my head swirled. I clutched the door as I stared into those dark eyes.

It was him.

I swear it was him.

I mumbled my top five artists — Taylor Swift, No Doubt, Pink, Selena Gomez, Aerosmith — before taking a massive inhale and then exhaled just as deeply. I looked again, and he was gone.

The monster was gone. Yet, I felt eyes on me. I turned over to look at Liam, whose kind smile was nowhere to be found. "What's wrong? Are you okay?"

After slamming the door shut, I fastened my seatbelt. "I'm fine, it's just... a minor flashback. I'm okay. Usually all I have to do is count my beads or list favorite songs or artists or books to calm myself. I'm fine now. Nothing to worry about." Was there? Was it really a flashback? That was twice now. It was so fast, but I'd swear it was him only older. This was different. This wasn't a flashback. It couldn't be.

Liam's brow furrowed. He acted worried and didn't appear to buy the episode was nothing to worry about. I considered trying to continue to plead my case, but instead we drove back to my house in silence. Like I said, it was great until it wasn't. Would I ever be normal again? Was dating Liam too much for my messed-up brain to handle?

EIGHT

CORA

I THANKED the couple and watched them exit the bakery. It was Ruby's first day working alongside me, and I admit it was nice to have an extra pair of hands. She wasn't in the kitchen yet, but she was great at greeting guests and making sure the tables were cleared and sparkling. She had cleaned the display cases and restocked fresh baked goods. And she had done it all with a smile and a gleam in her eyes. She was thriving outside of the house, interacting with new people.

Ruby was one of those people who dominated in social settings. An extrovert, someone who gained energy from being around others. I was so glad she would go to public high school and meet new people and have some friends other than her forced ones. I was a little worried at first about how she would adapt to so much stimuli, but seeing her in the bakery today, she was going to flourish in high school. Ruby was bright and friendly. Despite seeming clueless to the truth, I had the suspicion she understood more than she let on.

The poor thing had lived such a sheltered life. That wasn't good for her or anyone, really, but especially Ruby. I, on the other hand, did okay on my own and liked it, as long as it was my choice. Once someone takes away your choice, things you once enjoyed become your mental prison. I think Edison knew that, and it was why he had kept me hidden for so long. Not totally hidden. He allowed me to go to the grocery store, with a list approved in advance, and run other errands. Admittedly, without Ruby, I would have been pretty lonely. But she was growing up and would be at college in a few years, and it would leave me with only the bakery and Dorothy for conversation.

It would be okay. I wasn't someone who needed dozens of friends or to be in the spotlight. When I first met Edison, I liked that he took the reins on our activities. Like where we vacationed, who we spent time with, and where we would live. But when the rules were dictated, and he had done what he did, I realized I was living in a fantasy. The fantasy that I had free will. The moment Edison slipped that plain, gold band on my finger, he had taken mine away.

When I'd realized my mistake, I was in too deep. There was no turning back. A literal partner in crime. Most days, I shoved down the shame and carried on. After all, things were certainly different since he got his girlfriend or whoever she was. If I had known a few extracurriculars would buy me some freedom, I would have brought him a consenting woman home myself.

I often wondered what his girlfriend was like. Was she young? Married? Someone he worked with? Pretty? Did she know his secrets? I always assumed whoever she was, she had horrible taste in men. It takes one to know one.

Ruby bounced toward me. "How did I do?"

"You were brilliant."

"You think so?"

"You're a natural with customers. You are going to love high school." I hadn't loved high school. I was awkward and unpopular. Not a nerd, just plain and not into the normal activities like sports or alcohol. I should have known better when Edison, the star basketball player who could have had nearly any girl, had picked me to be his girlfriend our senior year.

"I can't wait. I have to admit, I feel full of energy. Like I swallowed the sun. Talking to people and asking them how their day is going — it's like, it's just how things are supposed to be, you know?"

"I do."

"When can I learn how to bake? I would love to bake. I mean, I know you taught me how to bake at home, but I mean like how to use the big mixer and the oven and the trays and the cupcake liners and how to decorate. Oh my gosh, I would love to learn how to decorate like you do!"

Ruby was aptly named. She was a jewel. Sparkly, beautiful, and creative. I was sure she would excel at decorating the cupcakes and even doing some of the cake designs as well. I would teach her over the next four years before she went off to college.

We were nearing the end of the day when the door opened, sounding the jingle bell. My body stiffened, thinking it might be Edison, but it was Liam. "Hey you. I appreciate the business, but, you know, I'm not sure eating a dozen cupcakes every day is good for you."

"Don't worry, I share them with coworkers. I don't eat them all."

"If you say so," I teased.

He glanced over at Ruby and stared at her for longer than I felt comfortable with. Liam wasn't one of those weirdos, was he? I hadn't been close with him since my sister, Liam's mother, and I weren't particularly close due to our age gap, and we'd lived up here most of his life. I said, "It's Ruby's first day of work."

He looked over at me and then refocused on the child. "That's great, Ruby. How did you like it?"

"It's so fun."

"Where's that friend of yours?" I asked, hoping that he liked adult women and not teenage girls. I would have known if my nephew was one of those, wouldn't I? He kept staring at Ruby like she was some sort of — I don't know what but it gave me a weird vibe. A worrisome vibe.

"Oh, she's probably still working. She works pretty much all the time. When she's not at home or working out."

"Is she your girlfriend?" Ruby asked with sparkling eyes. She was going to love all the high school gossip and drama.

"She's not, but I do like her that way. But..."

"But what?" I asked.

"She's adjusting to moving here and the new job, and I don't want to overwhelm her with a new relationship, too."

"Nonsense, Liam. I saw how she looked at you when you were here. She likes you."

"You think so?"

"I do."

The bell jingled, and I glanced over at my worst mistake. Ruby ran up to him. "Hi, Daddy."

He smiled and gave her a hug. "How was your first day?"

"It was great. I loved it."

Edison stepped back and unwrapped Ruby. "Good to hear. We need to get going. Grab your things."

I didn't know if Liam caught the fact Edison hadn't said hi to me, his wife. Liam said, "Hi, Edison. How are you?"

Edison looked Liam up and down. "I'm well, thank you. And you?"

"Well, thank you. You know, if it helps, I could drop off Ruby. I'm about to head home myself."

Edison faked a smile. It was creepy. "No, thank you."

"It's no trouble."

He grumbled, "I said no thank you. She's my daughter, and I will take care of her." The darkness had returned to Edison's eyes. Or had it always there?

Liam seemed startled and stuttered, "Sure, no problem." He glanced over at me, and I shrugged.

Ruby ran back out, having retrieved her stuff from the back room. She waved and headed out with her father. I said to Liam, "He's probably had a hard day. He has a tough job, and he is very protective of Ruby."

He didn't seem to buy the explanation. But what else could I say? *No worries, he's just a controlling maniac.* "What can I get you?"

"I'll have two red velvets, two peanut butter chocolates, and two pink lemonades."

"Somebody's hungry."

Liam chuckled. "They're not all for me. Red velvet is Allison's favorite, so I thought I would drop some off at her desk since she's still in the office."

"That's very sweet of you." As I collected the cupcakes for Liam, a twinge of envy filled me. I had once thought Edison was sweet and thoughtful, too. I had been so very wrong.

NINE

Staring at the vile creature in front of me, I almost felt sorry for him. It was almost six o'clock at night and I was having a one-on-one with my least favorite new employee, Marvin. I believed what Liam said was true, that Marvin was passed over for my job, and now it seemed he was hell-bent on making me pay for it. In the week I'd been at Troodle, he'd complained every day about either another department or something having to do with his workstation. Even the coffee in the break room. This guy didn't know who he was messing with. Did he realize he couldn't scare me away or annoy me into quitting? I was a person of action, not someone who would lie down and roll over. He should know better.

Was this job all he had in his life? Maybe that was why he took it so personally. He probably woke up in the morning and thought only about work and then came in and figured he could torture me *and* do his job. At least he did his job and was pretty good at it. As I threw insults at this man, in my head of course, I realized maybe we weren't that different. I mean, I never tried to make my boss's life a living hell, but I didn't have much outside of work, either. Maybe I should have compassion for him. Or maybe he should just get over himself and do his job and stop acting like a petulant child. I swear, I wondered if he just liked the sound of his own voice. It would explain why he kept droning on and on about this, that, and whatever other complaint he had. I shouldn't let him get to me. Marvin was the least of my worries.

It was late Monday, and I hadn't heard from Liam since our date on Saturday. He had me worried for more than romantic reasons. Now that he knew I was an attempted murderer, had PTSD, depression, and could snap and have flashbacks at any moment, what if he told people? What if Troodle found out and they fired me? What if I could never escape my past?

Now I was sure it had been foolish to tell Liam all my secrets. Well, not all of them. I still kept some for myself.

"It's not unreasonable, right?" Marvin repeated.

I wished I'd been paying closer attention or paying attention at all. I said, "Well, I've only been with the company for a week, but I think your input is valuable. If it's reasonable, we should come up with a plan." Vague, and he thought I was on his side. Whatever his side was. Maybe I could decipher what he had been droning on about with the plan.

"Okay, well, what's the first thing we should do?" he asked.

Oh, he was one of those? One of those employees who brings all the problems to the boss but with no solutions. In my experience, problems make a manager's job more difficult, not easier. I made myself rise through the ranks for a few reasons. One, I get along with people. Two, I'm good at my job. Three, before I go to anyone with a problem, I already have two or three suggestions on how to fix it. That way, I'd get a solution I want and it didn't put anybody out. Like a manager needs one more thing on their plate?

Marvin should know this by now. Then again, after our first

meeting, I went through his file, and it seemed he hadn't been promoted in quite a while, which was likely contributing to his lack of morale. "I think the first step is to brainstorm some ideas on how to solve this problem. Do you know how to do that?"

Okay, that came out a little snotty, but come on, really? Marvin had to be in his mid-forties and working for over twenty years. He should be able to handle a little problem solving.

"Yeah, like on a whiteboard."

"You can use mine. Let's do it together," I said with a smile, as if this was the joy of my evening. Not like I'd rather be having dinner at home, watching some good Netflix or hitting the treadmill or going on a walk or, really, absolutely anything other than sitting here with Marvin.

He stood up, walked over to the whiteboard, and picked up a marker, then looked at me. I said, "Marvin, you've been here a lot longer than I have, and I trust your judgment. What would be one solid idea to fix this problem?" Flattery usually worked better than negative energy.

Marvin nodded. "That's a good point. I think we should have guidelines around turnaround time for certain architecture pieces. For example, working with the single sign-on team. For such a simple request, the turnaround for that part of the diagram should be well within a week."

"I agree."

Marvin seemed to like that. His face lifted, and I swear he bounced. "Yeah, and actually, all pieces of the new architecture should have standard times for delivery, right? It would make everyone's life easier, especially on the project teams. And help our estimates be more robust."

He wasn't wrong. And it was a good idea. "Absolutely. You know, since you are an expert in this area, could you type this up in a document, like a standard procedure? And then send it to me, and I'll go over it with Bob and get his endorsement before communicating it to the other department directors."

He nodded and smiled. "Sure. Thanks, Allison."

"No problem. Nice work. Remember, my door is always open."

The door was not always open, but it's something managers like to say. As Marvin was leaving, past his shoulder, I caught a glimpse of a white paper bag with a pink logo and sparkling brown eyes. "Hey, Liam."

"Hi, do you have a sec?"

"Sure."

He came in and set the bag on top of my desk. "Peace offering?"

"What do you mean? I didn't realize we had any issues."

He sat down. "Let me start over. I don't like the way things ended on Saturday. After thinking it over, I realized I needed time to process everything. I don't know a lot about PTSD and these flashbacks you have. But I like you and would like to learn, if you're okay with that. Hopefully, you'll accept these cupcakes as my apology for being weird on our date."

Liam could be surprising. I'd give him that. Apologizing for *me* being a freak? "I forgive you. Actually, before I say that... what flavors did you get?"

Liam smiled. "Red velvet, pink lemonade, and peanut butter and chocolate."

"I accept your apology," I said with a smile. A genuine smile, and not one faked for the benefit of others. Oh jeez. Was my crush growing? Why wasn't he running away from me?

"Does that mean you'll go out with me again?"

He must be one of those people who found pain to be pleasurable. "I'd like that."

"Awesome. There are so many places I could take you. Do you like to hike?"

"Love it."

"This weekend, we could do a day hike to one of my favorite spots."

"Sounds great." Was he taking me to a secluded location? He was harmless, but was I?

"I could pack a picnic, and we could bring cupcakes if you like."

"I'd like that."

"All right, well, I should let you go. It's getting late. Have a good night, Allison."

"You too." My heart melted. Maybe I wasn't crazy after all. Maybe I was just new to this and I was overreacting. Dr. Baker told me the flashbacks weren't that serious. As long as I didn't attack anybody. Maybe it was the stress and new job, new house, new city, and new love interest. That would be a first. I'd dated, but I didn't know if I'd had a love interest. Like someone I really wanted to see. Even now, Saturday seemed far away.

I arrived home with some pep in my step and a belly full of cupcake. After a leftover pasta with meat sauce dinner, I sipped tea while watching *Stranger Things* on Netflix. At eleven o'clock, I yawned my way up to my bedroom. It was so quiet in the house, each step echoed through the halls.

After getting ready for bed, I lay down and melted into the pillow. I didn't realize how tired I was, but I was beat.

Four hours later, I woke in a cold sweat, screaming.

Another nightmare.

But this one was different.

In the dream, we were back in front of the grocery store. I was standing next to Josh, looking over at Ella, and I saw her struggling with the man. I ran and screamed and screamed. The man pushed her into the van. He smiled at me as he shut the door and hopped in the back with Ella before the van sped out of the parking lot.

How had I missed that detail?

It made sense now.

That was why it happened so fast. Why I couldn't save her. He wasn't alone. The monster had an accomplice. All this time, I thought it was only one monster and that he had run back to the driver's side and driven off. But logically, that didn't make sense because the van sped off within moments of Ella's screams while he was shoving her in the back. I needed to call Detective White. This could change everything.

TEN

I HAD LEFT messages for Detective White starting at six o'clock that morning. He needed to know there were two people who took Ella. The news reports described a manhunt for one suspect, white male, dark hair, dark eyes, and sharp chin. But the alerts to the public were wrong. I knew that now. The monster had an accomplice. Two perverted monsters stole my sister.

If I had remembered sooner, would it have mattered? Would a report of two people traveling in a white van be the detail needed for a credible tip from the public? Could we have found Ella if I hadn't gotten that detail wrong? Nearly tearing my hair out with frustration, I didn't understand why I hadn't remembered before.

Something was always missing from that event in my memory. And that's what it was. He didn't have time to run around to the driver's side. He jumped in the back, shut the door behind him, and they were gone. There was no way he would've had time to get behind the driver's seat from the back and drive off. He had an accomplice.

Not being able to get ahold of Detective White, I called Dr. Baker. She calmed me down and reminded me that the recovered memory was good news. But she was also concerned that since my move to Seattle, my fixation on Ella's case was heightening. Dr. Baker again suggested the stress of the move and the upcoming twenty-year anniversary of Ella's kidnapping were triggering all the memories and flashbacks. She explained major anniversaries were often quite triggering for family members and could easily explain the increase in symptoms.

That's what she said, but there was something in her voice that made me believe Dr. Baker wasn't telling me everything. Was it that she thought I could, in fact, be seeing the monster? It felt so real. Were age-progression hallucinations even a thing? Or was the impending twenty-year anniversary making me lose my freaking mind?

After the conversation with Dr. Baker, I was noticeably calmer, but I was still eager to talk to Detective White. It was eight o'clock, and I needed to hit the road and get to work. Figuring Detective White didn't need a fourth voice message, I grabbed my keys and headed outside. It was raining, of course. I ran to my car, got in, shut the door behind me, and made a mental note to break down the rest of the moving boxes and clear out the garage so I could park inside. Otherwise, every morning would start off wet. *No, thanks.*

When I was on the highway, Detective White finally called me back. "Hello, is this Allison Smythe?"

"Yes. Hi, Detective White. This is Allison, Ella's sister. She was kidnapped twenty years ago from Lafayette, California."

"Of course. I remember. How are you doing?" He asked it in a way that made me think he was suspicious of my current state of mind.

Was I talking too fast? "I'm doing well. I just moved to Seattle, and I've started a new job, and that's going great, but

I'm calling because I remember something new about Ella's abduction. There was a second person there. There was a driver. The man, the monster who grabbed Ella, with the dark hair, dark eyes, sharp chin... he wasn't alone. There was somebody already in the van." I explained my dream and how all the pieces fit together.

Tapping the steering wheel while waiting for a response, I wondered if the detective had given up on finding Ella. Everyone else had. I understood the statistics, but in my heart and my soul, I couldn't accept that she was dead and I would never see her again. I knew it was irrational, but I couldn't help it.

"We had considered he may have had an accomplice."

"You did? That was never told to my family, and it wasn't in the media."

"That's because we weren't sure, and we didn't have a description of the second suspect. We figured since we had a sketch from your eyewitness testimony, that would be enough to lure him out. It wasn't. And I'm sorry for that, Allison. I wish we could've brought her home. Ella's case is one that has stuck with me over the years. I know the twenty-year anniversary is coming up, and it's eating away at me we haven't found her."

He didn't even know her. If the case was eating him up, it had swallowed me whole. "Well, now that you know for sure there were two people, will that help?"

"Every additional detail will help. I will update the file and run some reports to see if there's any known suspects who work in pairs, like kidnappers and pedophiles, that kind of thing. I'll let you know if I find anything or if there are any new developments."

I was sure he remembered how I'd pestered the police for years and years and years, making sure they never forgot Ella. I hadn't stopped until the incident at the bar and the court-mandated therapy. Dr. Baker had suggested I stop obsessing about the case. She was sure if there was a break, the family would be the first to be notified. "Thank you, detective."

"You take care, Allison."

A little lighter, I ended the call and turned into the garage at work. Parked in the stall, I glanced in the mirror at my reflection. Dang it. I had done a terrible job on my makeup. It was obvious I hadn't slept for more than a few hours. I looked like hell. I needed to get my head on straight and manage my stress, so I didn't have another major incident. Keep calm and do my job.

After a deep breath, I cloaked myself in false confidence and dressed in my *woman who says all the right things and does all the right things* persona before jogging up the stairs to my floor. Using my badge to unlock the door, I put a confident expression on my face and walked toward my office. The cubicles were half empty. The other half were people who had probably been in since the early hours. Workers who had commuted from surrounding cities and got up early to avoid traffic. I set my bag down on my desk and headed over to the coffee machine. I pressed the buttons and slid a clean, Troodle-branded mug underneath the spout and nearly jumped at the sudden, "Good morning," that sounded from behind me.

I turned to my right, and Liam stood there with a warm smile. "Good morning," I said with as much cheer as I could gather. I felt manic, and I was trying to hide it, but something about Liam broke down my defenses. My armor didn't work on him and I wasn't sure how I felt about that.

"Is everything okay?"

"Everything's fine. I didn't sleep well, but I'll be fine after a big ol' cup of joe," I lied. It wasn't unusual for me to have nightmares, but same as with my other symptoms, they were becoming more frequent since I moved to Seattle. I thought it would bring me peace to be surrounded by the lush greenery and sparkling waterfront of Seattle, but I had been wrong.

"You sure?"

"I'll be all right."

"Anything I can do?"

"That's sweet, but really, I'm fine."

"What about lunch? I'll take you to lunch. I know this great little bakery that has outstanding salads, sandwiches, and cupcakes."

Baked goods certainly couldn't hurt. I smiled. "It's a date."

That made him smile even wider. He touched my arm, sending a tingling down my body as he said goodbye. After a quick moment of composing myself, I grabbed my coffee and headed back to my office.

LIAM and I laughed as we walked out of the building toward what was my new favorite bakery. Liam was becoming quite adept at putting me at ease and making me smile when all I really wanted to do was run and hide or hunt and fight. I wanted to find Ella, but what could I do? I felt helpless and alone, but somehow, when I was with him, it wasn't so terrible. Liam opened the door, and I stepped in, inhaling the scent of buttercream frosting and espresso. Sugar and caffeine, does it get any better?

Cora was behind the counter, and I waved. The café was busier than I had seen it before. Word must have been getting out that it was the best lunch spot around. Not that I'd been to many lunch spots, but Cora had me sold on the cupcakes alone. With only one table open, Liam pointed. "I can order if you want to grab a table."

"Sure. I'll have the Waldorf salad with chicken if they have it."

"You got it. Any cupcakes?"

Twist my arm. "If they have a red velvet, I'll take one."

"You got it."

I smiled as I walked over to the small bistro table and sat down. There was something about the bakery that drew me in. It exuded warmth like a big hug. Was it Cora? Or was it the happiness coated in cream cheese frosting? Or was it that I usually came here with Liam? Whatever it was, it was becoming one of my safe havens. Staring out the window, I people-watched as the masses passed by. Some were in a hurry, and some were strolling casually like they were on vacation. Despite the bumpy start, I thought I would learn to love living here. I simply needed to give myself time to adjust and calm my nerves better than I had been.

Dreaming out the window, watching the good people of Seattle, I cocked my head and stiffened when I spotted him. I sat up straight and leaned toward the glass. It couldn't be. It wasn't. As I stared at the man through the window with the dark hair now graying at the temples, dark eyes, and pointed chin, I knew it wasn't a flashback. I was seated. Sober. Calm.

He was real.

Through the window, I could tell he was twenty years older. With my heart nearly beating out of my chest, I turned my body to watch him as he advanced toward the bakery entrance. Eyes wide, my mouth dropped open ever so slightly. I couldn't believe it. It was him. This was not PTSD. This was the monster. Calming myself, I lifted my wrist and began counting the beads while I locked my eyes on him.

The jingle bells on the door sounded. He stepped in and turned right toward me. He looked away quickly but then did a double take and stared directly into my eyes. Recognition.

Frozen, my mind stopped counting the beads. He knew who I was. I lunged out of my seat and yelled, "It's you! You took her. Where is she?"

Liam rushed over to me. "What's going on? Are you okay?"

Without looking at him, I said, "No! I'm not okay. It's him. He's the monster!"

With his hand on my shoulder, Liam said, "Allison, no. That's not. Look at me." He tried to pivot me toward him. I gave in.

Wide-eyed, I said, "It's him," and turned back around.

Liam kept talking. But not to me. He said, "I'm so sorry, Edison. She has a disorder."

The monster relaxed, as if Liam had saved him. He said, "No worries," and smiled at me.

My nerves were firing off in all directions.

Liam said, "Let's sit down."

He guided me by the arm back to my seat.

"You know him?"

"That's my uncle. He's not a monster. He's married to Cora. Are you having one of your flashbacks?"

He grabbed my hands and looked me in the eye. "Breathe, Allison. Tell me, what are your five favorite artists? Will it help if I tell you mine?"

Liam thought I was crazy. I was not crazy. "Taylor Swift, Pink, Aerosmith, Selena Gomez, Kelly Clarkson."

"Are you better now?"

I turned around and watched the back of the man, Edison, as he exited with what looked like a young girl with long, strawberry blonde hair. I thought I might lose my breakfast. Calmer, and in more control, I said, "I'm okay now. I'm so sorry. Please apologize to your uncle for me." Uncle. The monster was his uncle.

"Good. You're safe. Okay?"

Was I? Cora walked over and sat my salad and cupcake in front of me and a sandwich in front of Liam. She said, "Is everything okay?"

The monster's wife. His accomplice?

Liam said, "Everything's fine."

Cora said, "Are you sure?"

I nodded without a word. Staring down at my salad and my cupcake, I couldn't move. I couldn't lift my fork, and I couldn't pick up the cupcake. This wasn't good. Liam needed to think I was fine.

ELEVEN

CORA

SHE SAID SHE WAS FINE, but I saw the look on her face when she spotted Edison. She recognized him. And it filled her with the fury of someone who knew what he was capable of. But what did she know? Thankfully, Ruby was still in the back and hadn't witnessed the scene. I didn't want Ruby asking questions I couldn't provide answers for. For whatever reason, she enjoyed her father's company. Well, I supposed the fact he mostly doted on her meant she could see him through a different lens. Small favors. At least Ruby was unharmed by his cruel and selfish nature. Not that she hadn't seen how he had treated me and his extensive list of rules that we all had to follow. Surely, that would leave an invisible mark on her. Hopefully, she understood it was wrong and didn't accept it as normal behavior.

I peered over at Allison and Liam. What did she know? She was not fine. I didn't know why she reacted the way she did. I didn't know all of Edison's sins, but I knew what he was capable of. Perhaps Allison was simply an excellent judge of character and sensed his aura was off or some new age thing like that.

I wish I'd had Allison's reaction to Edison thirty-five years ago when we had started dating. If I had seen him then for what he really was, I would have run screaming the other way. It would've saved me from a lifetime of heartache. Of terror. Of wondering what he would do with me when he didn't need me anymore. Would he kill me? Bury me in his back yard of secrets?

Part of me worried about what would happen to me when Ruby went off to college and she wasn't there as a buffer. It wasn't lost on me that Edison tried to be on his best behavior in front of her. But after she was gone, what would he need me for? Cooking and cleaning. He could easily hire that out, or he had several other options that didn't make me feel any better. I tried to look busy behind the counter, but I continued to watch as Liam consoled Allison.

Maybe there was something wrong with her. But what? Deep inside, a dark pit was growing inside of me. Had Edison done something to Allison? I knew he had done sickening things. Maybe she had been a victim. It had to be that. The look in her eyes would haunt my dreams. He had certainly done something awful to her. He didn't confide in me about every-thing he did, but he used to. Knowing Edison, he had done it in order to further torture me. To make me fear him. To be jealous of the attention he gave others. But he had divulged nothing in the past few years. That didn't mean he had stopped.

One could say I was complicit. I'd never told anyone. Even though I could have. Did that make me just as bad as him?

A middle-aged man wearing a Seahawks baseball cap approached the counter. "May I help you?"

"Yes, I would like a dozen snickerdoodle cookies, please."

"Anything else?"

"That'll be it. They're for my daughter and her friends. Snickerdoodles are her favorite."

"A special occasion?"

"No, she's having a sleepover now that school's out. I thought I'd surprise her."

Wasn't he a good father? Or was it an act?

"That's so nice. She sounds like a lucky girl."

He smiled, satisfied with himself.

I nodded, picked up a box, and headed to the case full of cookies. Stopping for a moment, I looked back over at Allison and Liam. Allison sat frozen as Liam took her hands in his. Allison had obviously been the victim of Edison's sickness — the rot that lived inside of him. He wasn't human. He was like a force that left a wake of destruction wherever he went. She clearly was not okay. How did she know Edison, and what had he done to her? Or was I better off not knowing at all? At this point with Edison, ignorance was bliss.

TWELVE

AFTER FAR TOO LONG, I finally calmed myself enough to think about this rationally. Initially, seeing him induced fear. But now I had a name. That meant I could learn what happened to my sister. But the only way to do that and not spook Liam or his uncle was to act normal. Like I had been mistaken. It was time to play the role of a lifetime. Like it did not disturb me that I was dating the nephew of the man who stole my sister. But I couldn't act too calm. It had to be believable that it was a response to stress. A flashback. I looked up at Liam. "I'm sorry, but I can't eat. I'll have to get this to go."

"Not a problem. But are you going to be okay?"

"I just need to take a beat. I'll ask Cora to pack this up and head back up to my office. I'll see you later, okay?"

"Let me walk you."

I supposed that wouldn't be a bad idea. Who knew what could happen in the short walk from the bakery back up to our office? What if Edison knew who I was? He could be waiting for me. I couldn't believe this was happening. I'd found him.

And he was related to Liam. What if Liam was in cahoots with everything his uncle had done? He had acted so strange when he saw Ella's photo on my fireplace mantle. Dread washed over me. What if Liam was his accomplice? Liam would have been eighteen. Young and impressionable. Maybe his uncle said, "Hey can you do me a favor?" And that favor was to help abduct my sister? Was it some sick game, befriending and dating me? Had he always known? Was Liam dangerous? I needed to think this through and come up with a plan.

"Okay."

"I'll get some boxes from Cora," Liam offered.

I nodded and sat there trying to think about what was supposed to be a fresh start was now crashing down all around me. The monster lived two doors down from me. How was that even possible? Do coincidences that big really happen? Something had brought me to that house. When the real estate agent showed me the property via video tour, I was drawn to it in a way that I couldn't explain. I had assumed it was the nature and the tranquil back yard. Maybe it was something more.

Liam returned and boxed up our food as I sat quietly. "It'll be okay, Allison."

"Thanks." But I didn't know if that was true anymore. I needed to call Dr. Baker and Detective White. This was a lot. But if I had learned anything in my thirty-seven years, it was to pretend to act normal, otherwise people would worry or try to get me locked up or worse. I gathered all my resolve and walked silently back to the office while studying each face that passed us on the street. Inside the building, I felt better. Maybe work was my only true sanctuary in Seattle.

At my office, Liam handed over my box. I thanked him, and he promised to call me later before I shut the door to my office. I set the food down on the edge of my desk, knowing there was no way I would eat it. Sitting in my executive desk chair, I turned and focused on my computer monitor to see what I had going on that afternoon. First, I skimmed my emails, but nothing was urgent. Then checked my calendar and saw I had an hour until my next meeting. Good. I pulled out my phone and dialed Dr. Baker. "Allison, what is it?"

"I saw him again. It was him. Not a flashback. When he saw me, he smirked. He knew it was me. Like he knew I knew he took my sister."

"It sounds like you need to take a deep breath. How about we do it together?"

Seriously? Was she not hearing my words? "Look, Dr. Baker, I know you think this is a symptom. But it's not. This is different from the other times. I'm telling you it's him. It's the monster."

"Okay, let's say it's the monster. Where did you see this monster?"

Had Dr. Baker always been so patronizing? "At the bakery. The man is my neighbor. He lives two doors down from me. He's Liam's uncle."

"Why are you so sure it's him?"

"I remember. The eyes and the chin. His hair has gray in it now, but it's him."

Dr. Baker didn't speak. Maybe it was a mistake to tell her. Was it going to be this difficult to convince everyone else, too? How would Detective White react? How could she not see this was different?

"Allison, I'm concerned about this. I'm wondering if you should stop seeing Liam and focus on yourself. It may be too much for you to handle. The move, the new job, the love interest, and the anniversary is a lot for anyone to handle. You need to take care of yourself. This could end badly."

"Are visions common in PTSD?"

"No," she said without further explanation.

If it's not PTSD, what is it? It's reality! Why doesn't she see this?

"Well, what do you think I should do?" I asked, a tad snippier than intended.

"Will they allow you to work from home?"

Work from home had been quite the rage over the last couple of years. I was sure if I said there was a family emergency, they wouldn't have an issue with it. Or I could simply say I wasn't feeling well and work from home. "I think that's a good idea. I can work from home."

"Good. Maybe you can visit with your mother and work from the Bay Area. Have you been doing yoga?"

Like yoga was a cure-all. "Yes."

"Good. Now, what is your plan for the rest of the day?"

Was I suddenly twelve and Dr. Baker was my mother? "I'm going to call Detective White and let him know—"

She cut me off. "You need to be very careful, Allison. This man you think is the monster may not be him. Do you remember when you thought James Hershin was the monster? He ended up in the hospital fighting for his life. Because you were wrong. I think you need to go home, have some tea, and do yoga or meditate like we've discussed before."

Obviously, I wasn't conveying this well enough. I was too hyper, not believable. Whatever. She didn't need to believe me. All I needed was for Detective White to believe me, and currently, the only thing keeping me from telling him was this conversation. "Okay, I'll do that."

"Where are you now?"

"I'm in my office."

"Can you go home? I think it's best if you go home."

"I just have a few more meetings today. I'll go home after that."

"Good. I care about you and don't want to see you going backward."

The conversation was pointless. She didn't believe me.

Annoyed, I said, "I appreciate that."

"This is very serious. If you continue to have these visions, I think it would be in your best interest to either go home and spend time with your mother or check yourself into a facility where you can get help. Another incident like what happened with James Hershin and I don't think you'll be given a lenient six-month hospital stay. We're talking about the criminal justice system, not to mention you could hurt another innocent person. Is that what you want, Allison?"

Of course not. Was Dr. Baker trying to get on my nerves? She said she was trying to help me, but she wasn't listening. Yes, I thought I'd seen the monster before, but now I knew I had. I turned on my confident, calm persona. "I'll be fine. Dr. Baker. I appreciate that. I'll take your advice and go straight home after my last meeting. I'll put on a yoga DVD and drink some tea. That sounds great, actually."

"I think that's smart. And if you feel you need to ask for help, that's good. You know what we say about that."

I rolled my eyes. "Yes, asking for help is a sign of strength."

"Exactly. You've been so strong. This is only a slight setback. Keep up the good work, and you'll be okay."

"Thank you." I hung up the phone, not waiting for any additional words of wisdom from my therapist. At least now I knew I couldn't talk to her about the monster anymore. How could she possibly think I'd lock myself up in a facility? That was crazy. No way. I searched through my contacts and called Detective White.

"This is Detective White."

"Hi, Detective, this is Allison Smythe."

"Hello, Allison. I haven't finished running the reports yet."

"That's not why I'm calling. I saw him. The man who took Ella. It was really him, and he saw me, and he acknowledged me. I found him."

"Okay, slow down and tell me exactly what happened."

After a deep breath, I slowly recounted the events from earlier in the day.

"Do you have his last name?"

That would be helpful, wouldn't it? "I can get it."

"On a scale from one to ten, how sure are you it's him? We've been down this road before, and it didn't end well."

"Ten. This isn't the same as before." I really needed somebody to believe me. Ideally, it would be Detective White. "What I know is that his name is Edison, and he's married to a woman named Cora and has a daughter named Ruby. Detective, I'm not wrong. It's him."

"You don't have a last name?"

Yes. I knew he would believe me. Detective White had always been kind and supportive. "I can get it."

"Call me back with his full name, and I'll check him out. Do a full background."

"Thank you so much, detective."

After the call, I felt a little better. I didn't know if Detective White fully believed me or not, but the fact he would do a full background check on Edison meant he was at least open to the possibility. Unlike Dr. Baker. All I needed was to get Liam to tell me his uncle's name. Glancing at the corner of my screen, I saw I still had a few minutes before my meeting. I wasn't sure of a casual way to ask Liam what his uncle's last name was. On second thought, it might arouse his suspicion if I asked him details about his aunt and uncle, and I didn't know if I could trust him. For all I knew, Liam was involved in all of it. I didn't need him to get the information. The monster lived two doors down. I could do a simple property records search and voila, the name of my sister's kidnapper would appear. My adrenaline pumped with this new lead.

Then I realized I may know where he lived, but he also knew where I lived.

THIRTEEN

With the home security installer out of my home, I breathed a little easier. After learning the monster lived two doors down, I wasted no time securing my home. What were the odds my new neighbor would be the vile man who had stolen my sister and our lives? Sometimes I hoped that if Ella was dead, he'd killed her right away and that she hadn't suffered long. I'd spent the last twenty years broken, with an enormous gaping hole in me. If she'd lived, she probably would have felt the same. I didn't wish that on her, or anyone, really. So, I guess I was selfish for hoping that one day I would see her again.

Despite my achievements, the only thing I ever wanted was for Ella to come home. All the other stuff was just distractions from what was missing inside me. Was that true of all over-achievers? Not trying to get too bothered with such depressing thoughts, I turned to the security system keypad and input the four numbers I had established just moments ago with the man from the security company. With a beep, the house was armed. Or was it? The security installer looked away when I created the code, but it didn't mean he hadn't somehow captured it.

With a few more taps on the keypad, I changed my security code and then re-armed the system. Was I safe now?

It would have to do. Rattled by the monster, I'd left the office after my last meeting and worked from home for the rest of the day. Maybe I would stay home for the rest of the week. At home, I felt more in control, plus it would allow me to work on my new side project uninterrupted.

First, I had to find Edison's full name and provide it to Detective White. After that, I needed to know more about Liam. I typically stayed away from social media as part of my recovery, but I could create a few fictional accounts and stalk Liam online. Who was he, really? He never said why he had moved from southern California other than the job opportunity. That was my line. So, obviously, he could be hiding something, too. Was that why he was so kind and forgiving of my symptoms? Or was it that he was checking me out for his uncle? Or was he a good guy, and I was so messed up I didn't know what that looked like?

I needed to call my mom. I usually texted her each day with a fun emoji and a "How are you?" or "Good morning." And I responded to her inquiries about the new job and town. I hadn't told her about the flashbacks or the sightings of the monster. Mom lost her husband six months ago and her daughter twenty years before that. I didn't want her to worry about me, and that meant she had to think I was thriving. Once I could prove Edison was the monster, I would tell her everything, but not before that. I would get answers for myself and for her.

She would still worry about me, but I didn't need to add to it. Mom told me she would come for a visit soon so she could see the new house. It was a thin cover for checking up on me to make sure I was safe and happy and not attacking strangers. Sitting at my desk, with my work laptop open, I called her.

She answered right away. "Allison. Are you okay?"

There probably wasn't anything that would make her stop worrying about me. "I'm totally fine. I'm just working from home today."

"Are you feeling okay?" She was such a mom — all the time.

"I'm a little under the weather. It's probably just a cold, but I don't want to spread it around the office. Anyway, I thought I'd see how my favorite mom is doing." It was a joke. Ella and I used to refer to our parents as our favorite parents. As if we had other parents.

"Isn't that sweet? I'm doing fairly well. Regina's over. We were just about to have tea."

Mom was much better at keeping friends than I had been over the years. All my normal behavior was just for show and rarely extended too much into my private life. Especially since most of my high school and college friends were married with kids. The social obligations had dwindled over the years, especially after my conviction. The last five years had changed everything. And if those years taught me anything, it was that when I suspected something to keep it to myself until I could prove it, and don't go at somebody's jugular.

"That's great. I should let you go so you can visit with Regina. Tell her I said hi."

"Okay, dear. I'll call you later so we can catch up. I want to hear all about what's new with you. All I get are those little texts."

"It's a date."

I ended the call and focused on my laptop screen. Thankfully, there was nothing too exciting going on at work. I even got Marvin to take control of what he perceived as the biggest departmental problem we had — people not following through with deadlines and providing their pieces of the project. At least one part of my life was under control.

On my personal computer, I pulled up a website to search for property records. It would alarm most people how quickly one can find such personal information with a few taps of the keys. I, of course, was no stranger to that concept, considering I worked in security architecture and was well-versed in all the different ways people tried to get into electronic files. But it wasn't just people with special skills who could dig up the dirt. Any old person off the street could search records and find out who owned a particular house. And that's not even the most sensitive type of information. With a credit card and a computer, you could know almost anything about a person. You name it, it's all there on the World Wide Web. Even people who are anti-Internet and think they live off the grid still own their homes. And property records were public in this day and age. There's nothing you could do to be completely off the grid. Unless you were born in a forest, and lived in a tent, and nobody ever knew you existed. Were there people like that? I didn't know, and neither does anybody else. But that's the point, right? A few minutes later, I stared at the screen and smiled.

Edison Carl Gardenia.

Gotcha.

A quick look over at my work computer to confirm nobody needed me, and I called Detective White. I provided the full name and address of the monster.

"I'll do a quick background check and let you know what I find. Are you doing okay up there?"

"I'm doing great. I have a new job at Troodle and a new house, that unfortunately is two doors down from a monster, but other than that, I can't complain." Not only that, but I had found the monster, and I would finally learn what had happened to my sister.

"If he is who you think he is, and he knows who you are, you could be in danger. What are you doing to stay safe?"

"This morning, I had a security system installed in my house. And I plan to be careful."

"If you get the feeling he's coming after you, you'll need to find another location until we can put him behind bars."

"Thank you, Detective White."

"You're welcome. You take care."

Detective White had been kind to my family since the very day that Ella was kidnapped right in front of me. As far as I knew, he followed up on every lead. I knew he still called Mom from time to time to let her know he hadn't forgotten about Ella. Even speaking to him now, I could hear the sincerity in his voice. He still wanted to find Ella just as badly as we did. Maybe not as badly. His life hadn't crumbled like ours had.

I wasn't a complete dreamer. Finding Ella didn't mean finding her alive. The chances of her still being alive after all this time were highly unlikely. But finding Edison made me believe we were one step closer to finding the truth. From the corner of my peripheral vision, I saw a chat box pop up on my work computer.

Of course. Liam.

> Are you here today?

He texted me last night and this morning, but I hadn't responded. But since I was online with my work computer, he knew I was around. I replied,

> WFH.

> You okay?

> I'm fine, just a cold. Don't want to spread it around.

> I'm worried about you.

Really? I'm worried about you and your kidnapping uncle. I didn't think I could trust Liam anymore. And didn't he know better than to have an "I'm worried about you" kind of conversation on a company-owned computer? Everything you type into a computer at work is an electronic record, owned by the company. Any email, chat, or other form of communication is captured and could be used in anything from a disciplinary review to a court of law. *Hello*.

> Not to worry. I'm taking cold medicine.

I wasn't, but how else was I supposed to respond?

> Okay. Feel better.

Finally.

> Talk to you later.

Was Liam covering for his uncle, or was he completely in the dark that Edison was a monster? He'd said he hadn't been in contact with Edison most of his adult life. Most wasn't all. And why did he act so strangely when he saw Ella's picture? It was time to learn more about Liam Parker.

Game on.

FOURTEEN

CORA

DESPITE NOT KNOWING what my husband may or may not have done to Allison, it had racked me with guilt since I'd seen the look on her face as she recognized him. I'd worried and pondered what he did to her, but the possibilities were endless. I decided to ask Edison about it and see if I could decipher his reaction. Of course, I'd be careful about my phrasing. Like, "It's so strange how she reacted. Do you have any idea why she freaked out like that? Have you met her before?" Hopefully, it went okay. He had been in a decent mood lately. I assumed that was on account of the mistress. But I had started to doubt my mistress theory. Maybe it wasn't one willing participant, maybe it was several or he was taking them by force. It wouldn't be the first time he'd taken what didn't belong to him. Unapologetically.

Edison wasn't a good man, but I didn't always know that.

I remembered when Ruby was born, and I was terrified of what he might do to her. But he treated her like a little princess and seemed to protect her from the outside world. He'd never once laid a hand on her other than a hug or a chaste kiss on her forehead. He'd never been inappropriate, which I'd been worried about. I put nothing past Edison. He was capable of the most vile and horrifying things people did. He had it in him.

I returned my attention to the stove. I had pasta cooking along with pans sauteing bison, zucchini, and onion for the sauce. Both burners were fired up when Edison stepped into the kitchen. "When will dinner be ready?"

"About fifteen minutes. How was your day?"

"Good."

My nerves rattled as I worked up to asking him about Allison. Edison did not like me questioning him about anything other than the most polite surface-level things like, "How was your day?" and "What do you think about this weather?"

I said, "Allison had a strange reaction to you at the bakery yesterday. So weird. Had you met her before?"

He smirked. "Allison. So that's her name. Never met her before. I don't know why she freaked out. Maybe she's mentally unstable. She looked that way to me."

He said it relatively convincingly. Maybe she was mentally unstable. Perhaps she was mentally unstable because of something he had done. "You've never met her before?"

"No, that was the first time. She's that girl Liam likes, right?"

"Yes, they work together."

"And she lives two doors down from us?"

I hesitated and wished he didn't know that. "Yes, that's right. She seems like a nice girl. I don't know why she freaked out like that."

He shrugged. "Maybe a case of mistaken identity."

His tone was even, and there was no surprise about why a woman would react like Allison had at the sight of him. I would think a normal, innocent man would be taken aback or even a little worried about it, but not Edison. I didn't think he was telling me everything, but just then, Ruby strolled in. "Hi, Daddy."

"Hi, Ruby." He put his arm around her. "You still like working at the bakery?"

"I do."

"Well, if you'd like, I can have you stay later, and your mom can drive you home from now on. But that's up to you. Is that too many hours for someone your age?"

This was most unusual. Was he trying to avoid the bakery? And Allison?

Ruby's eyes sparkled. "Oh, I would love to work more hours."

"What do you think, Cora?" he asked.

As if I had a choice. If Edison wanted me to do something, I had to do it. But in this case, I didn't mind. Ruby was a big help. And I knew she was excited to learn about how to bake at scale and decorate cakes. It had been fun having her around. She was like my apprentice. "Works for me. Of course, we'll have to change your hours when you go to school in the fall. But we'll cross that bridge when we get there."

Ruby hopped up and down, clapping her hands. "I'm so excited, and maybe during the downtimes you can start teaching me how to decorate. Maybe we can start with cupcakes."

"Absolutely. We can start tomorrow."

Edison's eyes squinted and turned dark. "I'll be in my study until dinner. Let me know when it's ready."

"Will do."

Ruby leaned up against the counter. "What's for dinner?"

"Pasta."

She leaned over the frying pan and saw the zucchini and onion. "Extra veggies?"

"Yep."

"Cool. Maybe after you finish teaching me about baking, you can teach me how to cook really well, too?"

"Sure. Any idea what you would like to do for a living?"

It would be too much to hope she would want to be a baker like me, and honestly, I thought that with her intellect she could do anything she wanted. Given the opportunity.

"I'm not sure. I love computers. It's because of computers the world is so connected. Like, I could talk to somebody in China or send them a text message in a matter of seconds. I always wondered how it all works."

Maybe her fascination stemmed from the fact computers were her only connection to the outside world until recently. It was how she was homeschooled and learned about the world. "Maybe your new high school has some computer classes."

"I hope so. Can I help?"

I nodded and handed the spoon to Ruby. She was sweet and loving and bright. I supposed she was born that way. For her sake, I hoped she did well in school and went off to college far, far away from him.

FIFTEEN

A FEW HOURS LATER, I was no closer to proving Edison or Liam had anything to do with Ella's abduction. After creating fake Instagram and Facebook accounts, all I'd learned about Liam was that he wasn't on social media much. His last post on Facebook was a year ago, and he had a few dozen friends. He didn't have Instagram, at least not under his own name. Was that weird? Maybe not, if he wasn't really into social media. I guess I would have been more surprised if he had been more active. After searching through the list of Liam's Facebook friends, I guessed one was his mother, and the others seemed strictly platonic. There were no kissy faces with girls or a relationship status. He was kind of like me. Was that good or bad?

My social media was essentially wiped clean after my conviction. Not a profile to be found. Had Liam looked me up and found nothing? Was that why he had reached out to a shared colleague before they hired me? I had been hiding something; that's why I stayed offline. Was it the same for Liam?

And I still hadn't heard from Detective White about the

background check for Edison Carl Gardenia. I hated just sitting around waiting for answers. Thankfully, I had my job to keep me busy. Truth be told, I had more work than there were hours in the day. Between trying to get up to speed with Troodle and meetings most of the day, I could fill every minute of the day if I chose. If I didn't have Troodle to keep me occupied, I thought I'd go mad.

Not that my mind hadn't drifted during department meetings. With my education and line of work, I knew there were other ways to learn about a person. I knew the back channels. And the front channels. And I knew people who were better at finding information than I was. People who may have more time than I did. People who couldn't be connected to me.

It wouldn't hurt to contact an old college friend to see if they had a few hours to spare on my account. One name came to mind. Henry. A great guy and friend. He was one of the few people who hadn't shunned me after the incident and my conviction. He'd reached out a few times to check on me, like a protective brother. Last I spoke to Henry, he hadn't changed a bit since college. It was nice to know some things never changed.

Henry barely slept and spent most of his nights crawling the deep, dark web. Not as a predator but as a hunter trying to take down the monsters. One night back in college, we were out at a bar, and he confessed to me, after a few end-of-semester shots of tequila, that he had messed with some financial records for a pedophile he had found online. To show me, Henry pulled up the news article of the man who went to prison for twenty-five years because of embezzlement and wire fraud. Henry told me they never found the child abuse materials on the criminal's computers. Apparently, he'd been smart and scrubbed his computers clean of the images but hadn't realized the financial irregularities and evidence of his financial crimes were still there. He was innocent of the financial crimes that put him away. Henry had laughed and said, "Nope. He wasn't guilty of that, but he was guilty of much, much worse things." He said it was his own brand of justice.

He was drunk when he told me about it, but considering he showed me the news article and explained how he had done it, I believed his story to be true. That night, we formed a bond. Nothing sexual. He wasn't my type. He was nice, introverted, and spent most of his time in front of the computer. But that night and that secret he shared with me was stuck in the back of my mind and quickly making its way to the front. Perhaps if I couldn't prove Edison Carl Gardenia took my sister in a court of law, we could bring him to justice in another way. Henry could help me out there. I owed him a phone call anyhow.

A knock on the door stopped my thoughts. I wasn't expecting anyone. Who could be at my house?

I rolled my chair away from my desk and hurried down the hall to my front door. Through the peephole, I could see it was Liam. He hadn't called. He hadn't texted. And he was just showing up at my front door. That was strange. Nobody did that. Why was he there?

Maybe he knew exactly who his uncle was and had been his uncle's accomplice. I did not know the truth at that moment, but I knew I needed to act normal, not like I was secretly plotting a special brand of justice for my sister in the event the police couldn't do so. I disarmed the alarm and opened the door. "Liam, what are you doing here?"

He held up a white paper bag with the pink logo. "I wanted to come by and see how you're feeling. I brought dinner."

We certainly weren't at that place in a relationship where he could stop by without calling and bring me dinner. I had known him for less than two weeks. And in that time, I'd learned his uncle had kidnapped my sister and probably killed her too. I didn't care what anybody said or thought; I knew it was him.

"How sweet of you. Come on in."

He stepped in. I shut the door behind him and rearmed the security system. I didn't know if Liam's visit was a ruse to distract me from my personal safety while his uncle was lying in wait two doors down, but I wasn't taking any chances.

We walked to my dining room, and he set the paper bag on the table. "I brought you a Chinese chicken salad and a few cupcakes. Cora came up with a new flavor that I thought you might like. It's a spice cake with cream cheese frosting and walnuts," he said with an apprehensive smile.

It did sound amazing. Well, unless he poisoned them. "Thank you, that sounds great. I'll grab plates and forks." And a knife.

"No need for plates. They come in the containers, but forks would be good."

I nodded, not averting my gaze from Liam as he set out our food and a box of cupcakes. Filled with conflict, I went to the silverware drawer and grabbed two forks and a steak knife I would say was for cutting up the cupcakes. Feeling so many emotions, I couldn't help but feel some sadness. I had really liked Liam and couldn't believe that he was connected to my worst enemy. And he had to know more about Ella than he had let on. His reaction to her picture was too odd. There was no way I could just forget it and move on. But the goal was to act normal because I didn't want Edison Carl Gardenia to see me coming for him. Next to Liam's dinner box, I set a fork and napkin and kept the others for me. "How's work?" I asked.

"Same old, same old. How is it working from home?"

"I'm working around-the-clock. It's like I'm always at work."

"At least you're feeling better."

"Yeah, I think I just had a bug. But I'll take it easy and stay home tomorrow, too. Hopefully, I'll be a hundred percent by the time Monday morning rolls around."

Opening the box, I studied the salad. Was it safe to eat? My fork hovered over my salad as I waited for Liam to take the first bite. "What did you get?"

"Same as you."

It was probably safe. I didn't see any markings on the boxes annotating one was poisoned and one wasn't. Looking at the cupcakes, I decided he could've poisoned those. I swear, my downfall *would* be in a baked good. I plunged my fork into the crisp lettuce and took a bite.

We ate in silence for a few minutes. I thought he could tell I was unnerved, and I needed to be more conversational, more normal. "Have you tried any new restaurants lately?"

"Not yet, but I was considering checking out a new Italian place this weekend and then maybe going for a hike after. If you're interested, I wouldn't mind the company."

Interested in being alone in the woods with a kidnapping murderer's nephew? "I'll have to see how I'm feeling. Maybe next weekend."

"I understand."

He set down his fork and placed his hands in his lap. "I wanted to talk about what happened at the bakery. I know we talked briefly right after it happened, but I just want to make sure you're okay. You seemed really freaked out."

"Oh, that. Don't worry. I talked to my therapist, and she's pretty sure it's just the stress of all the new things in my life, and the twenty-year anniversary is coming up, so there's a lot going on in my brain. She suggested I work from home for a few days to reduce my stress and work on my calming techniques. There's no need to worry."

"Do I stress you out? I'm a new thing," he said, with pleading eyes.

Damn, he could be charming. "Yeah, I haven't really dated in the last couple of years, and going out with you is fun, but it's new and kind of stressful. It's just normal dating jitters, but my therapist thinks it might be too much for me right now." I wished I hadn't said that because I didn't want to lose my connection to the monster. What about Cora? Did she know what her husband was like?

"Oh, I guess I probably shouldn't have come here then. I was just worried about you. You weren't answering my texts." He looked hurt as he started packing up his salad.

Was it a line, or was he sincere? Maybe he didn't know the monster his uncle was. His aunt must know. She was married to him. Or was he one of those killers who, when they're finally caught, their spouse, their children, their neighbors, and everyone else says they're shocked and just can't believe it's true?

"It's okay. I think we just have to take things really slow, if that's okay with you. I can totally understand if it's not."

He nodded. "Just for the record, my aunt says Edison is one of the best people she's ever known and that he's a great father and a great husband. So you have nothing to worry about with him."

Oh, really? I wasn't convinced, considering I'd seen the man with my own eyes. His face wasn't one I could forget. And trust me, I'd tried. "I appreciate that. Like I said, it's just stress. I'm fine. I promise." And then I managed polite conversation for the rest of the meal and thanked him for bringing me dinner, which, come to find out, hadn't been poisoned.

Still alive and kicking.

Was it too much to ask to find my sister and learn that Liam really was a good guy and not a secret spy for his horrible uncle? Even if it were true, could I overlook his familial connections?

SIXTEEN

Henry was just as I remembered him. Messy, jet-black hair. Intense dark brown eyes and wearing a hoodie and jeans, as if he'd never left college. From what he'd explained on the phone last night, he didn't leave his house very often. When I explained I needed his help with something, he said not to say anything sensitive over the phone. At first, it bummed me out. He was in the Bay Area. And I thought my plan failed, but like a super friend or a saint or something, he insisted on driving up right away to meet with me.

He had driven all night, and now he was at my house. How many people do you know that after phoning them for the first time in six months and asking them for a favor, they jump in their car and drive all night just to help you with some undisclosed thing? I could only think of one, and it was Henry.

"You didn't have to drive. I could have flown you up, or I could have met you somewhere." I didn't know where we would have met, but I felt like there was an easier way. Or I was still in semi-shock since he'd dropped everything for me.

He pushed up his large, dark-framed glasses. "Nonsense. I could use a change of scenery. I have a hotel picked out."

"You're welcome to stay here if you like. I have a guest bedroom."

"It's okay. You know me. I'm a loner."

That wasn't new. He looked around the house from the hallway. "Have you swept for bugs?"

Bugs? Did he think my house was dirty? I must have had confusion written all over my face.

"A sweep for listening devices?" he asked.

Ah. Of course. He was more paranoid than I remembered. But considering his hobby, maybe he'd gotten smarter about his covert activities. "No, I haven't swept for bugs."

He shrugged. "I figured." He took a device out of his backpack and without a word started roaming around my house with a black electronic device in his hand. "When did you get the security system?" he asked.

"Two days ago."

"It's probably okay. They're not likely listening. But just in case, we'll turn off the alarm while we talk, okay?"

I nodded.

"Actually, after I finish sweeping, I'll turn on my jammer."

"You've thought of everything."

He shrugged and continued through the house, looking for electronic listening devices. It would've helped if I explained I wasn't actually hiding out or under surveillance or suspected of a crime. I leaned against the wall in the dining room as I waited for Henry to finish. He trudged down the stairs. "It's safe. Nice house. You've done well for yourself. I'm glad you were able to put things back together."

Back together? I guess. "Yeah, it's actually what I wanted to talk to you about."

"It happened again? You can tell me."

From the outside, we were unlikely allies. But if I could trust anyone, it was Henry. "It's not that. But can I get you anything? Something to eat or drink? You had a long drive."

"Do you have cereal?"

I should have shopped. "I have granola."

"That'll be good."

He really hadn't changed a bit. I retrieved the granola from the pantry and the milk from the refrigerator and set them on the dining table in front of Henry before returning to the kitchen for a bowl and spoon. "Any coffee?" I asked.

"Yes. Thanks."

Henry was usually a man of few words, which was why his drunken confession about his little hobby had been surprising. I fired up my Nespresso and made him a double. If I remembered correctly, he lived on caffeine, cereal, and candy. I didn't have any candy to offer, and I felt bad about that. He'd driven for twelve hours. I could have gone to the grocery store.

After I placed Henry's coffee in front of him, I asked, "Are you sure you don't want to stay here? You saw the guest room. It's nice. You'd have your own bathroom," before sitting across the table from him.

He set his spoon down, as if reconsidering.

"Please stay here, or at least let me pay for your hotel. You are helping me. Let me do something for you."

"Okay. But I might need to get back tomorrow. I can probably stay longer, depending on whatever it is you need me to do."

I owed him big time. "Thank you so much, Henry. I didn't know who else to turn to. Whatever I can do to repay you, name it."

"Nonsense. You said it was something only I could help with. I figured it was major."

I picked up my white porcelain coffee mug and sipped the bitter brew. As he ate his cereal, I explained everything that had happened since I'd arrived in Seattle. From the first sighting to the confrontation at the bakery.

Henry's eyes were wide and magnified by the large frames on his face. "He lives two doors down? That's a pretty big coincidence."

"I know, but stranger things have happened, right?"

He nodded and continued eating his granola, with each bite crunching and crunching.

"Anyhow, so I told Detective White — he's the original detective on my sister's missing person's case. I gave him Edison Carl Gardenia's name and address. He said he would do a background on him but..."

"But you want to know everything."

"Yes. I want to know everything. Like who he is, where he's been, and I need to know about Cora and Liam, too. I need to prove it was him, so I can make him tell me what happened to Ella. I have to know."

He lifted his hand, as if to stop me. "Allison, I will learn everything about this man and his wife. And this Liam, too. I'll tell you everything that has happened since the day he was born. I'll find everything that has an electronic record. Don't worry, okay?"

"Okay."

"Shouldn't be too hard. What did you say he does for a living?"

"Liam said he's an insurance executive."

"I bet he does a lot of business trips. That is promising."

"Thank you, Henry. I don't know how I can ever repay you."

He finished the last bite of granola, picked up his coffee cup, and took a sip. "You're one of the few good people I know.

That's why after what happened, when you were in the hospital, I wanted to reach out to let you know that you're a good person and that you deserve all the happiness in the world."

My nose tingled, and my eyes teared up. Henry never ceased to surprise me. It wasn't a romantic love or romantic admiration. He truly saw me as a friend. I needed to be better about visiting with him and reaching out to him, not just when I needed something. "I appreciate that."

"I need to finish up a few things for work, and then I can get started on this."

"That's great. What are you doing for work these days?"

"Cybersecurity," he said with a devilish grin.

I chuckled. "Is that right?"

"Yeah, people pay me pretty good money to hack into their systems. You know, I think you could do it, too. If you are ever so inclined."

In college, I had gone through a hacker phase, probably because I was hanging out with Henry too much. It was kind of fun to see the different loopholes, but of course, trying to be normal and maintain my overachiever status, I had to go the legit route. Not that what Henry did wasn't legit. Companies needed his services to make sure the bad guys didn't come in. He likely conducted an assessment and then communicated to the company the system's weaknesses so they could fix them. I considered that type of career before leaving college but opted for the corporate world, living in the light instead of the shadows, like Henry. Plus, I wanted Mom and Dad to be proud, and I wasn't sure they would understand the job and would maybe fear I was an underground type. But it was a good job and paid well. If I was being totally honest, it would be too easy to get lost in my thoughts if I were alone all day. Being around other people helped me forget. Helped me avoid. "I'm happy at Troodle."

"If you change your mind, let me know."

"I haven't done that kind of work in a long time. I mostly manage people and review architecture diagrams, my security team's plans, and project upgrades for existing systems."

"Boring."

I chuckled again. "You're not wrong."

"I'm gonna get to work. Thanks for the granola."

"You can work in the guest room. It's upstairs on the left. Or you can work down here on the dining table. Whatever you prefer."

"I'll work in the guest room."

"Can I get you anything from the store? I could pick up some provisions. I don't have any candy," I said with a smile.

"No candy? How do you live?"

"Cupcakes," I said, sheepishly.

"The bakery where you saw him?"

"Yes. I've been avoiding it ever since, but I thought I should go back and act like it was no big deal. I don't want him to think I'm going after him. I want to pretend like everything is okay and I was having an off day."

"A surprise attack."

Henry was skilled at getting past computer security systems, as well as my false exterior. "Exactly."

"Smart."

Finally, someone who believed me. "What can I get you from the store?"

"I don't want to be a bother."

"I have to go, anyway."

"If it's not too much trouble... M&Ms. Reese's Peanut Butter Cups. Red Vines. Coke. Captain Crunch. Bagged salad. Any flavor is fine."

I cocked my head.

He shrugged. "I eat vegetables now."

"Good to hear. I'll go after my next meeting. The pods for the espresso machine are in the cupboard above. My house is your house." I was about to head back to my workstation when Henry put his hand on my shoulder. "We're going to get him."

I certainly hoped so.

SEVENTEEN

CORA

IT WAS AN UNUSUALLY slow day at the bakery. Probably because it was a Friday and people left work early to start their weekend. Those folks who had active lives and enjoyed their loving spouses and families and had fun places to go and people to meet. Most people's worlds weren't like mine. After thirty-five years with Edison, I didn't have a single friend except for, well, Dorothy, but she didn't really count. And she probably secretly hated me. I guess Ruby was the closest thing I had to a friend, but she was so young and didn't understand the world yet, and I certainly couldn't confide in her about what was really going on. Although I suspected she understood more than she let on.

That was why I loved the bakery so much. It enabled me to talk to adults, even if it was mostly small talk. But I was getting a few regulars, and the polite exchanges had turned into a discussion about their families and children.

Financially, the bakery was far from breaking even, but it was ahead of projections. I took a lot of pride and satisfaction in that. The bakery had all-around improved my quality of life. After Ruby went off to college, it would be my entire world.

Ruby propped her elbows up on the counter and rested her chin on her fists. "What do we do when it's really slow like this?" Ruby asked.

"We can clean up, organize, and check inventory. Or we can think up new recipes to try." Her eyes lit up at the last suggestion. Not surprisingly, cleaning and inventory weren't exciting activities. "We should come up with new cupcake and frosting combos. Any ideas?"

Ruby cocked her head. "Maybe if we sampled some of the existing flavors, it would spark ideas for some new ones."

She was clever, that one. Nobody could ever tell her she wasn't. "Let's do it." We would have plenty left over at the end of the day. We didn't sell day-old cupcakes, so I had tried to convince Edison to let me donate them to homeless shelters. But he didn't like me going too many places without him. An hour before closing, I tried to give them away to customers, or we brought them home. They never went to waste. Although I think I gained a few pounds since we'd opened. Thankfully, Edison didn't notice, or he simply didn't care.

The shop door opened, and a familiar face greeted us. "The whole bakery to myself?"

I said, "Yep. It's all yours, Liam."

He glanced over at Ruby with a strange expression on his face. They hadn't met until a few weeks ago. Neither seemed to be terribly interested in the other, not negatively. It was more that he was an adult male and she was a teenage girl. I'd be more worried if they were interested in one another. "Ruby, how do you like working here?"

"I love it. We were just talking about coming up with some new flavors."

"What have you come up with so far?" Liam asked.

"None yet, but maybe a chocolate cake with marshmallow topping and graham cracker sprinkles? Like s'mores. But a cupcake."

"That sounds great. I'll take a dozen."

I said, "We'll have to write that down. It could be a hit." I walked around the counter. "What can I get you, Liam?"

"One of your best cupcakes and a turkey club to go."

"Ruby, why don't you pick out a cupcake for Liam, and I'll get started on the sandwich."

She nodded, and I headed over to the cooler and grabbed the fixings for Liam's sandwich. I set them down on the counter and began preparing the sandwich when I said, "I haven't seen Allison in a few days. Is she okay?" I hoped I didn't seem overeager to learn what Allison had reacted to, but I was curious to know what Liam knew about it.

"She's fine. She's been working from home."

"Oh, good. I was worried after she was here last time. She seemed really freaked out."

Liam hesitated. "She's going through a difficult time right now. The stress seems to have triggered some flashbacks. And mistaken identity. It's not the first time it's happened."

"Flashbacks from what?" Ruby asked.

"I'm not sure if she wants me to talk about it, but something bad happened when she was much younger, and the anniversary is coming up. Plus the stress of the house and the new job."

"Where did you say she was from?" I asked, as if I didn't remember.

"California."

"Whereabouts?"

"The Bay Area."

"She thought Dad was somebody else?" Ruby asked.

Lord, please say it's not true. Not that I deserved the Lord's grace for all the things I'd done. I had no right to ask, but please let me just get through these last four years with Ruby and then things would be different. Then I could expose his secrets if I had to, but not with Ruby still at home. When she found out, she'd be hurt, but at least she'd be away from him. And I didn't even want to think about what would happen to me. I hoped it didn't come to that.

"Yes. But she now knows your dad isn't a dangerous man."

Or did she? I said, "How scary. The poor thing."

"I hope she's okay," Ruby added.

"She is. It freaked her out as you could imagine, but she says there's nothing to worry about, and she plans to be back in the office on Monday. So, expect to see her then."

"Good to hear. She seems to like cupcakes," I added, trying to act normal and not completely relieved that Allison didn't believe my husband was the person from her past. Hopefully, that meant Edison hadn't done horrible things to her. But it sounded like somebody had. Maybe Edison looked like Allison's bad man, or she could feel the same dark vibes in him. I prayed that's all it was.

Liam smiled. "Cupcakes, coffee, and computers. I'm pretty sure those are her three passions."

"Computers?" Ruby asked.

"Yep. She's the Director of Financial Systems in the IT department. She's a solutions architect by training but has been quite successful and is now a director."

It entranced Ruby. "That's so cool."

The two started talking about computers, and I tuned out, concerned about more pressing matters, like whether my home and my family and my life were about to crumble.

EIGHTEEN

Dressed and standing in my kitchen at the crack of dawn, I had hardly slept. Spending most of the night tossing and turning, hoping Henry had found something we could use to prove Edison Carl Gardenia had taken Ella. I was trying to play it cool, but I was itching to find out the truth about what happened to Ella and then find her. And make sure I was not actually crazy. My mind kept going back and forth, asking myself, was it really him? I swore it was. I hadn't imagined the smirk and the wink and the overall sleazy vibe.

But my rational brain asked, how did he recognize me after twenty years? I was seventeen when we last locked eyes. I was now thirty-seven and looked older and a little heavier. And I was in Seattle, not in the Bay Area. Maybe he was just an icky old man and he was flirting with me? Gross. But a possibility, I guess. Maybe he didn't know I was Ella's sister, but he had taken her.

The more I thought about it, the more I doubted myself. Considering I had been so sure the man in the bar was the monster who took Ella, too. This was different, wasn't it?

Turning on the coffee machine, I waited for it to heat, hoping Henry would give me the news soon. But if he was like he was in college, he was a later sleeper or hadn't slept at all. I shoved in a pod and pressed the small cup icon. It filled up, and I inhaled the dark roast, wondering if the caffeine was what I needed or something in my stomach. While the coffee filled my cup, I grabbed a banana from the counter, peeled it back, and took a bite of the sugary-sweet goodness. After devouring the entire thing, I realized I must be hungrier than I thought.

Grabbing the coffee and downing it in one shot, I picked up the glass of water on the counter and took a hearty gulp. After glancing around the kitchen, I didn't know what to do with myself. I couldn't go for a walk in my neighborhood, knowing that the monster was two doors down. There was always work to be done. A footfall on the hardwood made me jump. Henry gave me a sleepy nod. "I hadn't expected you up so soon."

"Up?"

"Did you sleep at all?"

He shook his head. "I just came down for coffee."

I pulled out a pod and grabbed a small mug from the cupboard. "How's it going?" I said, even though I was afraid to ask. I didn't want to seem pushy, but he had to know all of this was weighing on my mind.

"So far, I have found nothing, but that doesn't mean I won't."

Nothing? There's no way he was clean. "What did you check? His financials, property records, employment records..." I felt bad after I said it. Henry knew what to look for.

He grabbed the coffee mug, now full of espresso. "I did a standard background. He's clean as a whistle, from what I can tell. But like I said, I'll keep digging. I have to go back to the Bay Area today, so I may get on the road in a few hours. But I'm not giving up. We're going to get him."

He didn't seem as convinced as he was the night before. Had I imagined it? Was I losing my mind? Maybe it wasn't him. Was I grasping at straws? Freaking out about the upcoming anniversary? Was Dr. Baker right? I didn't like that. And I couldn't help but question my memory. Detective White once explained to me that eyewitness accounts were highly unreliable. I had pushed down that knowledge, but it was rearing its ugly head. I knew I hadn't gotten a long glimpse of the monster when he took Ella. He was about twenty feet away when I saw him and he saw me. Our eyes had met. Squeezing my eyes shut, I tried to push out the terrible memories. The man grabbing Ella as she screamed, and him throwing her in the back of the van before climbing in and shutting the door while the van had moved.

Henry stepped toward me. "Are you okay?"

"I was so sure it was him."

"Well, then it probably is, and we'll find the evidence. We'll make sure it sticks."

"What if I'm crazy? What if I only saw what I wanted to see?"

"Something is triggering your memories and your night-mares. Maybe that man is the monster. He could act smug because he thought he had gotten away with it. But here you are now. Maybe he's shaking in his boots, scared. He might even try to run."

Henry said that for my benefit. I didn't think Edison was running anywhere and wasn't likely to be afraid of me. He must have been unconvinced himself, since he said, "I'll keep digging. I'll look at dates around Ella's kidnapping and try to cross reference it with his travel. It'll take some time. Employment and housing records are easy, but plane flights, travel, and rental cars will take time. I have to check all the different rental sites, all the different airlines... you know what I'm saying. It's a lot of work. Don't give up yet."

Had I sent Henry on a wild goose chase? He and Detective White seemed to be the only ones who understood what I was going through and not patronizing me but legitimately trying to help me. "What if I'm wrong?"

"Do you think you're wrong?"

I shook my head. "I think it's him."

"Then don't doubt yourself. I'll sort this out. As soon as I find something, I'll come back. Okay?"

"I hate to put you out."

"Don't even think about it. I don't have a lot going on. There are a few things I need to do this week in the Bay Area. It's unusual, actually."

How could there be people like Henry, so kind, so generous, and then there were people like Edison Carl Gardenia, who would snatch a teenage girl out of her sister's car and never bring her back? "Breakfast?"

"Sure."

I fetched the cereal and milk and brought them over to the table. Over breakfast, I asked him about his hobbies outside of vigilantism. He told me he was working on a video game, and he had a presentation for some investors, which was why he had to head out. Henry had two jobs, one as an entrepreneur and one as a freelance security consultant, yet he still dropped everything for me. I was so happy for him and wished there was something I could do to help him. And it sounded like he had an online community that he was quite active in as well. From the outside, it seemed like he was a hermit who never left home, but he had created a life, perhaps even better than most. That made me feel better to know he had friends and was thriving in his own way. Good things should happen to good people.

A few hours later, he had his backpack on, with his laptop case under his arm.

"Thank you so much."

"That's what friends are for."

I wrapped my arms around him and squeezed him tighter than I'd squeezed anyone in a long time. "Thank you. I don't know how to repay you."

"Enough of that. I get to have you as my friend. That is thanks enough."

He was too kind. Did I deserve it? I disarmed the security system and opened the door.

"Now, make sure you always have that on when you're home, okay?"

"I will." I waved and shut the door. Henry had made me feel better about what I saw, and that it was the monster and I wasn't going nuts. Kind of.

NINETEEN

I REREAD the same paragraph three times. As much as I tried to keep my mind on work, it kept drifting back to my conversation with Henry. I had heard nothing from him since he left, which meant he had found no dirt on Edison Carl Gardenia. Which meant I still hadn't proven that I wasn't crazy. I could be crazy. Most crazy people don't know they're crazy.

If anybody could find something on Edison, it would be Henry. I certainly couldn't wait for the police to bring him to justice. They'd had twenty years to find him, and they hadn't identified a single suspect until now — and the tip came from me. Maybe it wasn't their fault. Detective White probably had ten other cases he was working. It wasn't like the police department could afford a team of investigators for twenty years for a single missing person. I wasn't unsympathetic to their limitations, but it didn't mean I had to stand back and do nothing.

A figure in the doorway drove me back to reality. It was Marvin. *Great.*

"Hi, Marvin."

"Are you feeling better?"

"Much. Thank you. Is there something I can help you with?"

Without asking to enter, he strolled in and sat down, which was fine, considering my open-door policy. And the door was open and there was an empty chair.

I wondered what Marvin was like outside of work. Did he have a family? Friends? Did he kidnap young girls?

He said, "I sent you the proposal for the terms of service for the project team members last week. Is it possible to get your feedback today?"

Right. "I'm so sorry I haven't gotten to it yet. I started reading it, but I keep getting distracted by meetings and phone calls. You know how it is." I hesitated. "Did you have a good weekend?" If you pretend like you care about employees' lives, they will be more loyal and work harder. I learned that in a management seminar. Not that I didn't care about my employees. It was more that I didn't think we needed to discuss the details of our home life at work.

He gave me a blank expression. Was he shocked I was being friendly? If so, I needed to work on that. He then said, "Yeah. My wife, kids, and I road-tripped to Cannon Beach and spent the night."

Mind blown. "That sounds amazing. How old are your kids?" People love talking about their kids.

"Eleven and nine."

"They must keep you busy."

He nodded, and his posture relaxed. "Do you have kids? Are you married?"

Part of me was relieved that he did not know my background because that could mean nobody else did either. But in my gut, I was thinking if Liam could figure out my background, surely the rest of them could. Maybe nobody else cared and

nobody else looked me up. If that was true, why had Liam?
"Nope, it's just me."

"What prompted you to move to Seattle?"

"The job and the change of scenery."

"Well, if you need any recommendations for things to do in the area, I'd be happy to help."

Maybe I had been wrong about Marvin. He seemed nice now that he wasn't threatened by me. A normal guy with a wife and kids. Maybe he was just trying to do the best he could for his family. In some ways, he kinda reminded me of my dad. "I appreciate that. I'll put the TOS at the top of my priority list, but it may take until tomorrow."

"Tomorrow would be great. Thanks, Allison."

Marvin was no dummy. He knew this terms-of-service procedure for the department could make him look good across multiple departments and possibly get him a promotion. Maybe not in my group because I had the next level up, but perhaps it would open up his opportunities to be a director in another group. And despite the chilly reception when I first joined, Marvin was warming up to me, and he was growing on me. I returned my focus to the computer and read the paragraph, finally comprehending what it said.

A knock on the door frame. "You busy?"

Why people asked that when we're always busy was beyond me, but I let it go. Considering his eyes were sparkling and his dimples were on full display. "Hey, Liam."

"Hey, I was wondering if you wanted to grab lunch today?"

I had to remind myself to act normal and not like he was the nephew of my mortal enemy. "Oh, sure. What do you have in mind?"

"Well, there's the bakery."

He must've sensed the change in my demeanor, because he said, "He won't be there. If that's what you're wondering. Cora told me he no longer picks up Ruby from the bakery." He stepped into my office and shut the door behind him. "I was thinking, if you think it could help your recovery to actually meet him face-to-face and have a conversation, I could introduce the two of you. I'm sure Cora would help set it up."

Normal face, normal reaction. "I don't think that's necessary. I'm fine. Really. But I think lunch at the bakery will help normalize the location for me. Go back to the scene of the crime and see there is no crime."

"Okay. See you later."

I waved as Liam exited my office.

After shaking off the feelings about Liam, I returned my focus to work, only to get another private phone call. At this rate, between the personal conversations, the phone calls, and working from home on week two, I was surely going to get fired any minute. I looked at my phone and picked it up. "Hello."

"Hi, Allison, it's Detective White."

"Thank you for calling me back."

"We did a full background on Edison Carl Gardenia. He has no priors and a clean criminal history. As far as we can tell, he has lived in the same house for thirty years and has worked for the same company during that time. I don't think it's our guy. Maybe he's someone who looks a lot like him."

It was possible I was wrong.

The walls were closing in, and I shook my head and took a breath.

"Allison, are you still there?"

"Yes, thank you for looking into this. I appreciate it. He must be somebody who looks like him."

"If this happens again, call. We will find him one day."

Shutting my eyes, I said, "Okay, thank you, Detective White," and ended the call.

"Detective?"

I opened my eyes and glanced up. Marvin had returned. "Oh, hi, Marvin." I set my phone down on my desk.

"Are you talking to a detective? I'm sorry. I hate to interrupt."

Well, you just did. Another bonding moment? "Yes. No worries. Our call is over now."

"I hope everything is okay."

Everything? More like nothing. No, that wasn't true. Some things were okay. "My sister was kidnapped almost twenty years ago. They never caught the man who did it. That was the detective on her case. He still keeps in touch with me and my mom to let us know he hasn't forgotten about her."

Marvin placed his hand over his chest. "I'm so sorry. I didn't know."

"Thank you. It's been a long time, and some days are harder than others." Being vulnerable with employees was good. And it didn't need to be a secret. My sister was kidnapped. That I thought it was Liam's uncle was a different story. Or that I had flashbacks or suffered from depression and PTSD and was on medication and talked with a therapist. None of that needed to be public.

"Oh." Marvin lowered his voice before walking closer. "I had a cousin who went missing. She was thirteen, adorable, fun-loving, and smart. For a long time, the family held on to hope that she would be found alive, until they found her body. My aunt said it was better to know than not know, but she said sometimes she wished she could still picture her out there. She said she missed having hope."

"They tell me I have to... accept that she's gone."

"Never give up hope, Allison. Until they tell you she's gone, don't give up. During the time they couldn't find my cousin, my aunt and uncle spoke with many families whose children went missing. My aunt and uncle met other families who had been reunited with their missing children ten, even fifteen years later. They found them. Alive! I'm not saying the children were totally okay or that they didn't have problems, but they were still alive. Never give up hope."

He tapped my desk with his hand and walked out. Staring at his back, I shook my head. I hadn't expected that. Remembering he must have come into my office for a reason, I called, "Marvin."

He turned around.

"Was there something you needed?" I asked.

There was sadness in his eyes. Remembering his cousin's death? "It can wait."

I nodded.

An unexpected ally. At last, I had found one person in this universe who didn't think I was delusional for not giving up hope I would see my sister again. I was with Marvin on this one. Until they showed me her dead body, or her dusty old bones, I would never give up hope.

TWENTY

My HEART RACED as Liam and I approached the entrance to the bakery. I thought I'd be fine and could wear my calm and unaffected mask, but the memory of Edison standing there with a smug look on his face, as if he were untouchable, made me sick to my stomach. It was as if he knew exactly who I was and he enjoyed my pain. He probably did. Liam stopped and said, "Are you okay? We can go somewhere else."

Apparently, there were several cracks in my mask. I needed to work on that. I told myself it would be okay. He would not be there. It was just lunch. And cupcakes. "It's okay. I'll be fine. There isn't time to go somewhere else because I only have an hour." I was never more happy to have a meeting right after lunch.

"If you're sure."

"I am." I was. That monster had taken enough away from me. He would not take away cupcakes, too. Plus, I wasn't afraid of him. Not really. What could he possibly do to me? He'd nearly destroyed me mentally, so who cared if he tried to physically harm me? Not that I thought he would. There would be too many questions now. I had to keep telling myself I had the upper hand because if I was right about him, I did. If I was wrong... well, then he'd have no reason to come after me, and they'd probably lock me up again. I was fine. *Totally fine.*

Liam opened the door. "After you."

Great. I sucked in my fears and ambled inside. Cora was behind the counter and nearly all the dozen tables were filled with people munching on cupcakes, cookies, the occasional salad, and sandwiches. Based on the people in line waiting to order or pick up, Cora was doing a pretty good take-out business. The bakery was only open Monday through Friday, obviously targeting the work crowd that surrounded the bakery. Lots of worker bees with only a few minutes to pick up lunch and bring it back to the office to eat at their desks.

We advanced in line. Cora smiled. "Allison, Liam, good to see you."

I said, "You too." Was it true? Did she know her husband was a monster? Did she help him? Was I surrounded by the family who had stolen my sister?

"What can I get you? Your usual?"

I had a usual? Maybe she was referring to the Chinese chicken salad. "Actually, I would love to try the green goddess salad today."

"Excellent choice. And you, Liam?"

"Chicken pesto sandwich."

She punched a few keys on the register, and Liam handed over his credit card. Cora said, "I'll bring them right over. Take any table."

We thanked her and chose a table near the window like the day I saw him. Studying the room, there was no sign of the monster. There was no threat. I was fine. I was in control, and I was going to get the goods on Edison. And Liam and Cora. I would learn the truth. And then justice would be served. My preference would be that all responsible for Ella's kidnapping would rot in jail for the rest of their lives. But if that couldn't happen, I had Henry. My dependable and too nice of a friend, Henry. Although I had to admit I was worried since I hadn't heard from him yet.

We sat in silence as I recalled my conversation with Marvin. How I had confided in him about my sister and how he'd been one of the few people to tell me not to lose hope. You just really never know about people. Here I had thought Marvin would be an adversary, yet he was an ally and, who knew, maybe even a friend one day. Telling Marvin about my sister didn't feel strange, which I thought indicated some kind of progress. I used to avoid speaking about it. Maybe I should be more open about it when asked or even offer it up when in a conversation that allowed for the topic to come up naturally. Dr. Baker had suggested, since the beginning, that talking about what happened would help me heal, which would lead to acceptance.

Even if I could accept, the guilt would never go away. It was my fault. I had left her there to talk to a stupid boy. If I hadn't done that, Ella and I would have grown up together and maybe even have led stereotypical lives with picket fences and wedding bands, all the while being best friends.

Cora brought out our lunches and what looked like free cupcakes. Was she really capable of helping a monster? Either way, I had to act normal and apologize for the last time I was there. If for no other reason than to appear like the event was no big deal. Cora said, "Ruby invented a new flavor. It's a s'more cupcake. It has chocolate cake with marshmallow frosting topped with toasted graham cracker crumbs."

"Can I skip the salad and just eat the cupcake for lunch?"

Cora laughed. "You can do whatever you want."

"Thanks, Cora. And, since we have you here. I wanted to

apologize for what happened before. I promise it will never happen again."

She waved it off. "Liam explained everything. There is no reason to apologize. I'm just sorry that you had to go through that." She glanced over her shoulder to see the new group of customers who had just come in. "I have to get back. Enjoy." She hurried away.

Liam said, "I was here when Cora and Ruby invented the flavor."

"Maybe you inspired them." I was flirting. Ugh. Why did he have to be related to the monster? It had been so long since I actually liked a man.

Despite my proclivity to eat the cupcake first, I filled myself with sustenance and healthy food before enjoying the baked goods. I learned over the years that although junk food was good in the moment, it didn't make me feel any better in the long term. I ate mostly healthy, but I loved cupcakes and ice cream and cookies. One a day wouldn't kill me, right? I dug into my salad. I polished it off and made my way over to the cupcake.

Liam said, "Are you doing okay? We've been here for a while now."

Was he overly concerned about this? "You can stop worrying about me. I am perfectly fine, I promise."

"Are you sure?"

Was he pressing because he was getting information for his uncle? Why was he pushing so hard? I said I was fine. I was fine. We weren't in a place in a relationship where he could question me. That kind of irked me. Good, I needed to like him less. I gave a weak smile. "I'll let you know if I'm not fine, okay?"

"I'm sorry. I didn't mean to push. It's just that I care about you."

After the last bite of cupcake, I just smiled and picked up my purse. "You ready to head back?" Without waiting for a response, I pushed back my chair and stood up.

"Uh, yeah."

I stepped toward the exit, and Cora hurried over. "What did you think of the cupcake?"

Feeling full of hope and sugar, I was about to speak, but then she appeared.

Frozen in time, I stared at my sister. Ella.

The girl spoke. "Did you like the cupcake?"

Stunned, I couldn't reply to the young woman. Young. A teenager. It couldn't be Ella. Ella would be thirty-four now.

"Five out of five stars," Liam said.

"How about you? Did you like it?"

"Allison?" Cora asked.

I stared at the girl. Her sparkling blue eyes and long strawberry blonde hair with peaches and cream complexion.

Cora said, "Where are my manners? Allison, this is my daughter, Ruby." She glanced at her. "This is Allison. She's our neighbor and a friend of Liam's."

"I heard all about you. You're a computer architect, right? I'd love to learn about that. It's so nice to meet you."

My head swirled. Steadying myself, I said, "I'm so sorry I have to go back to work. I have a meeting, but it was great to meet you."

I waved but didn't move. I couldn't take my eyes off her. Liam tapped me on the shoulder. I waved again and hurried out of the bakery. He followed me outside.

I turned and stared at Liam with tears forming in my eyes.

Liam said, "I can explain." He put his hand on my arm.

"Don't touch me."

I shook my head and ran. I didn't know where I was going, but

I knew I had to get away. Pushing my way through the crowds, I ran until I found a semi-private spot down a side street. Out of breath, I leaned up against the wall of a building, slid down to my bottom, and wrapped my arms around my knees. Was I losing my mind? That couldn't have been Ella. It was Ruby. A fourteen-year-old girl. Not Ella. But she looked exactly like Ella. How could that be? A doppelgänger? Some article I once read said we all had a carbon copy of ourselves out there somewhere. Was Ruby Ella's doppelgänger? It was possible. But it was too coincidental, wasn't it? I could see that. *Oh, god.* I was losing my mind. Was Dr. Baker right? Did I need to check myself in?

I squeezed my eyes shut and curled my hands into fists. Anger flushed through me. Liam knew Ruby looked like Ella. That must be why he had acted weird when he saw my sister's photo. He knew that his cousin Ruby looked exactly like Ella, and he said nothing. Why didn't he warn me?

My thoughts were swirling like a tornado as I tried to make sense of everything. I *couldn't* make sense of it. I tugged off my beaded bracelet and began counting the beads until I had made my way around the whole thing twice. That was when my phone buzzed in my pocket. Realizing it might be work, I pulled it out. Mom. I had never called her back. I sat up and answered. "Hello?"

"Allison? Are you okay?"

"I don't know, Mom, I don't know." Tears streamed down my face, and I shook my head. Had it all been in my mind?

"What's going on, Allison? What happened?"

After I poured out everything I had been keeping from her, Mom said, "Allison, it's going to be okay. But I think you need to go home. Call a ride share or a taxi and go home. I'll book a flight and come up — today. You don't have to go through this alone. We'll fix it together."

Shaking my head, I said, "I don't know, Mom. What if I can't be fixed?"

"It'll be okay, honey. Call Dr. Baker when you get home. I'm booking a flight as soon as we hang up."

"You don't have to do that. I'm okay. I'll call Dr. Baker."

"Call me as soon as you finish talking to her, okay?"

"Okay." I ended the call and was about to call Dr. Baker when I realized the time. I was late for my meeting, and I couldn't exactly stroll in looking like I did. I went into the email app on my phone and emailed the organizer, saying I wouldn't be able to make it. It would be rude not to. Composed, I stayed put and called Dr. Baker from my current spot. Once she answered, I gave her half a second for pleasantries before I blurted out what had just happened, including the phone call to my mom.

She said, "Allison, I agree with your mother. I think you need to go home or if you prefer, and I would feel better about this, you could check yourself into a facility where you can get some rest. I have a few places I can recommend. Have you slept?"

Like through the night? Not in twenty years. And I didn't even know if I had before that. "I slept a little."

"Okay, I think you need to get some rest. If you don't want to go to a wellness facility, it would be a good idea for you to visit your mother instead of her coming up to you. It will help to be in a familiar, safe place. Like your childhood home."

"Okay. That sounds like a good idea. I'll book a flight back to the Bay Area."

"Where are you now?"

I moved away from my phone and looked around me. People were looking at me like I was nuts while I sat on the street. I couldn't say they were wrong. After I wiped the tears from my cheeks, I said, "Near my office. But I'm going to grab my things and go home."

"That is a good idea. Please call me when you get there."

Defeated, I said, "Okay." I couldn't believe I had been so wrong *again*. It was only my mind playing tricks on me. What did this mean? Would I lose my job? My new house? My independence? Shaking off the terror that my world as I knew it may end, I stood up and dusted off the back of my trousers.

TWENTY-ONE
CORA

ALLISON SPED out of the bakery as if she'd seen a ghost. I
turned to look at Ruby, and my heart nearly stopped. Maybe I
was making too much of this. She couldn't possibly know our
secrets. It was impossible. At least that's what I told myself. I
was being paranoid. Understandably, I thought. Ruby said,
"What was wrong with her? She sprinted out of here like she
was on fire."

"She said she was late for a meeting."

Ruby didn't seem satisfied with that. Sometimes I had
wondered if she was too smart for her own good. I was
suspecting I was right about that. "Is she normally like that? Or
do you think she was having one of those episodes Liam was
telling us about?"

I certainly hoped not. "Normally, she's friendly. I think
she was just late for her meeting." Did I really believe that? If
it was my worst fear, how could she possibly know? Maybe
she was a psychic? I wasn't sure I believed in all of that, but
just because you don't believe in something, that doesn't
mean it doesn't exist. It would explain her reaction to Edison

and now Ella. It was the only logical, yet illogical, explanation.

"Is she Liam's girlfriend? Or are they just dating?"

How did Ruby know the difference? Had she gotten past the parental controls on the internet? "I don't know. But I know he really likes her."

"I think it's so cool that she's a solutions architect, a female engineer. And a director too. Do you think she'd sit down with me and talk about her job? Like mentor me, or at least talk about what it's like to be female in that field and how she got to be such a success."

"She probably would. She seems like a nice person."

"We could entice her with cupcakes."

"I'm sure that would do the trick." But did I want her to be around Ruby? What if Allison knew something? Like because of her secret powers or whatever was causing her reaction to my family.

"Can you ask Liam to ask her for me?"

Unsure of how to explain I didn't want Ruby to spend extra time with Allison, I said, "Sure, no problem."

Maybe I was being silly. Psychics? I was sure it would be harmless. All Ruby wanted to do was to talk about computers, and I certainly couldn't help her there. I couldn't shelter Ruby forever. But how would Edison react if he found out? I knew how he would react. He had sworn he'd never seen Allison before, but I wondered if it was something worse. Or something recent, like Allison had witnessed something he had done — and Ruby was with him. And that was why she had reacted so strongly to the both of them. Had Edison done something to Ruby?

Four more years. I needed four more years and Ruby off to college, and then I could rid myself of him. I didn't even think he would care if I left him if I kept my mouth shut. Would I lose my bakery? Maybe. But I could start over. I built one, I could do it again. If I didn't go to jail, too. With the mental reminder that I needed Ruby to go to college, I not only should allow, but I should encourage Ruby to talk to Allison, right? If Ruby wanted to pursue computers as a job, having a mentor like Allison could help her and ensure that Ruby went away to college. She deserved that. And so did I. But I needed more time to think about it.

"Thank you so much!" Ruby stared at me with pleading eyes.

"What? You want me to call now?"

"Well, business is slow..."

I couldn't argue with her logic. And I didn't have any excuses to postpone the decision. Maybe Allison was too busy to meet with Ruby, and I didn't need to worry about it. And Edison didn't need to know. Considering he no longer picked up Ruby from the bakery, it could be Ruby's and my little secret. When had my life turned into one secret after another? I could no longer remember a time when I told the full truth.

Smiling to hide my anguish, I took my cell phone from my apron and texted Liam.

> Ruby was quite taken with Allison. Would you mind asking Allison if she would meet with Ruby and talk to her about her career? Ruby is interested in learning about engineering. Maybe they can have lunch?

After a breath, I pressed send. "Okay, it's done."

Approximately thirty seconds later, Ruby said, "Has he replied yet?"

"Not yet."

Ruby gave a half-grin, but she had an odd look in her eyes that I couldn't quite figure out. It was like the look her father made when he was planning something. Something I'd rather not know about. Had I been wrong about Ruby? Had she inherited her father's darkness?

I had seen no signs of cruelty. She loved cats and all the neighborhood creatures. No, she couldn't possibly have his darkness. She was too kind, and I didn't think it was an act.

Perhaps all this business with Allison was twisting me all up. First, Allison's powerful reaction to Edison and now Ruby. Something wasn't sitting right with me, but what?

I watched as Ruby trotted back behind the counter. She began pulling out cupcakes and setting them on the counter. "What are you doing?"

"When Liam responds, tell him we have a box of cupcakes for her. We can give her one of each flavor. What do you think?"

That Ruby was innocent enough to think you could buy someone with cupcakes. "I think it's a great idea."

Ruby smirked. She was definitely up to something, but I wasn't sure what. Maybe she saw Allison as an opportunity to get away from us. I knew she wanted more than we'd given her. After raising her in a bubble, she wanted the rest of the world. It was understandable. Maybe she saw Allison as being part of that. If that were true, what was the dread growing inside of me?

TWENTY-TWO

BACK INSIDE MY OFFICE, I was filling my bag with my laptop, notes, and other things I would need to take home. The more I thought about it, the more I wasn't sure what the right thing to do was. I could visit Mom, but I certainly would not check myself into an inpatient facility. If I did, I would surely lose my job and unnecessarily worry my mom, although I had already done that. So, what would I do? There was something wrong with me. But putting me in a mental hospital wouldn't fix that. Maybe I just needed less stimuli. Maybe my job choice was no longer right for me. Henry had offered me a lucrative career choice. One where I didn't think my coworker's uncle kidnapped my sister. It was something to consider. It would be less stressful, and if stress was contributing to my symptoms, then a less stressful job was what I needed. And I could move back to the Bay Area and be close to my mother and the few friends I had left. After all, Mom was the only family I had.

As soon as I was home, I planned to call Mom and let her know I was fine and not to jump on the next plane to Seattle.

Ruby was not my sister, I knew that. I'd be fine, and I didn't need any help. All I needed was to destress my life. That's all.

The move had been a wrong choice. I was woman enough to admit my mistakes. It was a simple enough fix. It wasn't like I needed to turn water into wine. A remote job and to sell the house. A few phone calls, that's all it would take. After a few momentary setbacks, I would get back on track. It would all work out. I would survive the twenty-year anniversary of Ella's disappearance, and then I would try my best to move on. The storm would pass, and I would survive. My phone buzzed. Speaking of.

"Hi, Mom."

"How are you doing, sweetheart?"

"I'm much better. There's no reason for you to hop on a plane. I'm sorry I freaked out and scared you. I have a plan now. A plan to destress and then the symptoms will subside. I know Ruby isn't Ella. She's just a girl who looks a lot like her. She doesn't even have freckles like Ella. I'm not going crazy. I promise."

Was that a thing you could promise?

"Are you sure? I can imagine seeing someone who looks like our Ella could be quite unsettling. Oh, dear."

"Mom, I'm okay, I promise." I would be. Just not yet.

"If you don't want me to come up, then I think you should come home. Just for a little while. I'm sure your work would be understanding."

"I'm fine. I'll be okay. But I do plan to work from home for the rest of the day. And maybe even for the rest of the week."

"Are you home now?"

"No, not yet."

"Call me when you get home. I want to know you're safe."

"I'll call you when I get home."

Mental note: call Dr. Baker and Mom.

After about an hour sitting on the street, calming myself, and then returning to my office, I felt like I had flipped a switch and gone back to being a normal person. I probably didn't need to work from home, but it had been a stressful day, and I should take some time to destress and consider a new life plan. One where I didn't hallucinate. I would take the afternoon to get myself sorted and be back the next day.

Dr. Baker was overreacting, thinking I needed to be hospitalized. I was just fine. I'd be fine. A knock on my door drew my attention to a visitor.

"Come in."

The door opened, and it used every bit of energy I had to look pleasant and normal and not a sobbing mess.

Liam walked in and said, "Hi," before shutting the door behind him. "I wanted to check on you. You ran off before we could talk."

"I'm fine. I was just startled. Ruby looks so much like my sister. I know she's not my sister. It's not a flashback. I just needed a moment. Really. Even I know there are differences in their appearances. I'm sure there's plenty of people who look like my sister, actually. And besides, my sister would be thirty-four now. I'm sorry for freaking out like that, but I just needed some time alone."

The worry remained in his eyes. He wasn't buying it. But he could suck it. He could have prevented my freak out if he'd simply told me his cousin looked so much like Ella. He stepped closer. "I'm really worried about you."

"That's unnecessary. I mean, I appreciate it, but there's nothing to worry about."

"Well, it looks like you're packing up."

"It was an emotional day, and I'm heading home. This whole thing is kind of silly, actually. I mean, come on. One day, I'm sure I'll look back on this and laugh," I said, playfully, as if it was no big deal that I had practically seen the ghost of my fourteen-year-old sister.

"You're sure?"

"No more worrying. I'll be back at work tomorrow," I said, believing it myself and that Dr. Baker was wrong, as was everybody else. These were just momentary setbacks, minor incidents, really.

He nodded. "Okay." He started to say something and stopped.

"What is it?"

"Oh, this may not be a good time."

I sighed, tired of being handled with kid gloves. "I swear I'm fine. Anything you throw at me, I can handle." It wasn't true, but he didn't need to know that.

"Well, I had talked to Ruby about you, and I told her you're a solutions architect by trade and that you're a director at the company, and it really impressed her. She really likes computers and thinks that she'd like to go into engineering. Ruby asked Cora to ask me if you'd be willing to have lunch with her to talk about your job and what it's like to be a solutions architect. But maybe it's too much, considering..."

Saying no would make it seem like I wasn't okay with the fact that Ruby looked so much like my sister. Could I handle it? Maybe it would help because then I could reprogram my brain to know that she was not Ella, and that she was Ruby. An actual teenage girl interested in engineering. That certainly wasn't Ella. Ella was more of the artistic type who loved to draw and paint and took pottery classes. We were like opposites. Yin and yang.

"She's offered cupcakes."

I smiled my best. "If there're cupcakes, I'm in."

"Are you sure?"

"I'd be happy to." What could go wrong? I could have a

full-on meltdown and collapse in the streets of Seattle and cry my eyes out. Been there. Done that. I survived and got the T-shirt. No, I was stronger than everybody thought I was. I could spend a lunch break with Ruby and talk about engineering without freaking out.

"All right then. I'll let Cora know. Thank you. And I'll see you tomorrow?"

"I'll see you tomorrow."

He exited and shut the door behind him. I'd miss my new office and my new house. But I knew I couldn't continue like this. I had tried to be unaffected by what happened, but I was drained and needed a new life and maybe a nap. Only problem was, if I fell asleep, what would I dream about? As soon as I shut my eyes, I'd be thrown into the nightmare of running toward a screaming Ella who was being dragged into a van and not being able to save her.

TWENTY-THREE

AFTER SOME HERBAL tea and a yoga video, I felt centered and ready for the next chapter of my life. Confident I could handle seeing Ruby, who looked too much like Ella, and I could even handle seeing Edison because I knew he wasn't Ella's kidnapper. Didn't I? Did I? I mean, I conceded Ruby wasn't Ella, obviously. I had admitted the man in the bar wasn't the kidnapper. But the only thing that had changed about my opinion of Edison was that I thought there were too many coincidences for him to be the monster. Maybe I needed to see him again, to be sure. He couldn't be fully exonerated — not yet.

As I waited for Zoom to boot up, I contemplated how I could get a look at Edison again. Within moments, Dr. Baker's beaming face stared back at me on the screen. I smiled and waved. "Hi, Dr. Baker."

"Hi, Allison. You seem like you're doing a lot better."

"Yes. I did some yoga and drank some tea. I worked from home this afternoon, giving myself some time to adjust and recoup from my earlier feelings."

"I'd like to talk about what happened earlier today. Are you okay with that?"

"Sure."

"Walk me through exactly what happened when you saw this girl, this teenager, who looked like your sister."

Keeping my composure, I calmly explained, "I met Ruby, who is Cora's daughter and Liam's cousin. The resemblance to my sister surprised me, and I found myself quite startled. I know that there are people out there who look like us, like a doppelgänger. But to see this young woman who looks so much like Ella, I felt surprised and sad because Ruby is fourteen, just like Ella was when she was kidnapped, and I'm sad that Ella's not here anymore. I'm still grieving, Dr. Baker."

"Yes, you've been grieving for a long time, and to be honest, you may never stop grieving completely, and that's normal. It sounds like you accept that Ella's not coming back."

I nodded, although it wasn't true. Did I think there was a huge possibility Ella was still out there? No. But was it possible? Yes.

"However, over the past few weeks, you've had two hallucinations. You've now seen a girl who you say looks identical to your sister. These events, factored in with your previous diagnoses of PTSD and clinical depression and the actions that you took against the man in the bar, make me think I might have missed something."

That didn't sound good. Like something was even more wrong with me?

She continued, "It's not uncommon for PTSD patients to develop additional psychosis such as schizoaffective disorder. I know it sounds a little scary, but I think we should evaluate you for this disorder. It could help you because then we could put you on the right medication and tailor your therapy to help you cope with these situations."

Was she saying I was schizophrenic? This was not good news at all. Were they going to throw me into a padded room and keep me drugged up all day while my mother worried that I might murder somebody? Although, to be fair, I did almost kill a man, but I was drunk and hallucinating. I knew Ruby wasn't Ella. I knew her chin was different, but her eyes and her hair and her skin complexion were very similar.

I nodded again to let her know I was listening. Not that I agreed with her. Dr. Baker stared back at me with an expression of sympathy and encouragement. It was the look you would expect a mother to show her three-year-old child after they'd made a mistake like drawing on the walls and then Mommy would say something like, "We draw on paper, not on walls. I know you can do it."

Did I even need therapy anymore? Nothing had improved since I'd been going to Dr. Baker. All we ever discussed was my stress and my symptoms. And until the last few weeks, I had none of them other than the continued guilt for not saving Ella and for what I did to that poor man. I did everything I was supposed to. I wasn't schizophrenic.

Dr. Baker said, "What I'd like to do, if you're okay with this, is to have you visit so we can evaluate you."

"Like in the Bay Area?"

"Yes. And I can tell you're not convinced that you have schizoaffective disorder, and you may not. I'm just saying it's a possibility. And if we don't treat it properly, it can lead to additional issues. For example, does this sound familiar? Schizoaffective disorder includes symptoms related to losing touch with reality. Those symptoms include delusions, hallucinations, disorganized and confused thought patterns and speech..."

As she spoke, I wondered if she really thought I was sick. Maybe if that was the issue, I could take a pill and be fine?

She continued, "... typically, people first exhibit signs

between the ages of sixteen and thirty, but another risk factor linking schizoaffective disorder to PTSD is the experience of trauma. You have experienced trauma, and as your doctor, I cannot ignore the delusions and hallucinations added with the attack on the man in the bar. I need you to come in so we can do a full evaluation."

Staring blankly at the screen, I knew I wasn't delusional, and I hadn't lost touch with reality. I knew exactly where I was. Dr. Baker was wrong. I owned a home and held a job which proved I was a high functioning individual. "Well, now is not a very good time. Can't we just do this over a Zoom call?"

"We could start there, but it's best to evaluate you in person."

"Dr. Baker, I'm going to be honest with you. I don't want to lose my job, and I fear that if I leave now to be evaluated for psychoses down in California, that I could lose my position I've only had for a short time."

Not that I wasn't already contemplating leaving and moving back to California. But Dr. Baker didn't need to know that. And I simply didn't want to go get evaluated. I wasn't a threat to myself or others. She needed to back off. And I was nixing these daily check-ins. I didn't need them anymore.

"Could you ask them to let you work from home?"

"I'm working from home, but I can't work in a hospital setting. I lead meetings, and I have employees who count on me."

"I can't force you to do anything, Allison. But at least promise me you'll take a small break. I am concerned that if we don't treat this, something terrible could happen, and I know you don't want that."

"I just spoke with my mother, and I plan to fly out Friday night to visit." It wasn't true, but if it got Dr. Baker off my back, it was worth the fib.

"Friday is four days away. Will you be able to wait that long?"

Dr. Baker was getting on my nerves. If she was so concerned and so great at her job, why didn't she properly diagnose me five years earlier when I had slit a man's throat? That was the time to determine if I had some sort of schizoaffective disorder. But I was sure I didn't have it. I wasn't hallucinating or having delusions. I knew what I saw. "It'll be fine. I'll keep myself in a calm and stress-free environment."

"I'm glad to hear that. Why don't you check your calendar and find out when you can come to California for an evaluation? It'll probably be several days. Plan for a week. Best-case scenario, we have nothing to worry about and you don't have these psychoses. The second best scenario is that you have this, and we put you on the right medication. Third is the worst scenario, and that's we don't evaluate you and you have it and we don't treat it and something bad happens."

"I'll look at my calendar."

"Okay. Be sure to send me those dates."

"Thank you, Dr. Baker." I left the Zoom meeting.

I didn't feel great about lying to Dr. Baker, but come on. Seattle wasn't my forever home, but I wasn't leaving without learning more about Edison Carl Gardenia. Maybe during my meeting with Ruby, I could learn more about her dad. Maybe she knew something that would give me clues I could pass to Henry for his investigation. There was no way I was leaving Seattle yet. Dr. Baker could suck it.

TWENTY-FOUR

Startled awake by a terrible realization, I nearly jumped out of bed. Up at an ungodly hour, I hopped on my computer and began researching serial murderers. What I found is that they often chose their victims based on similar traits, whether it be physical or personal characteristics. And with that information, the last puzzle pieces completed the picture. The coincidence was no coincidence. And I was going to prove it. But in order to do that, I couldn't have Dr. Baker harping in my ear, saying that I was a psychotic person because I thought I may have located Ella's kidnapper. I'd prove her and everyone else wrong.

And I had a hunch Ruby would help me do just that. I didn't like the idea of using a child, but I thought of it more like a mutually beneficial situation. Ruby would learn about solutions architecture, my time in college, and my experiences rising up the ranks in the world of software development, and she would share information with me — about her dad. I would infiltrate her young mind and break down her defenses to get her to open up about her father and what he was really like. I was convinced more than ever that Ruby would be the key to unlocking the truth about Edison Carl Gardenia.

No more breakdowns, no more second-guessing.

This was real.

My phone buzzed, and I glanced at it. After a solid eye roll, I ignored the second call from Dr. Baker. I had told her the day before that I didn't need daily check-ins and that our normal weekly schedule was all I would commit to. She'd acted concerned and said we should check in every day until I could be diagnosed and treated. Seriously? If she really thought I was dangerous, and she hadn't cured me in the last five years, what could she do now? She seemed to be intelligent and have my best interest at heart, but now I really had to question that.

She had no justification for me to fly home and to put me into a mental hospital again. And I looked it up online. She has no basis for involuntary confinement, either. As far as I was concerned, Dr. Baker would either keep me as a patient and talk once a week, or I would fire her. I didn't have to see her anymore. It was my decision how often we checked in, not hers.

I had work to do, a job and a life to lead, and most important, above all else, I had a man who needed to be brought to justice.

Stepping inside the bakery, I smiled brightly and waved at Cora. "Hi, how are you today?"

"I'm doing well, and you?"

She gave me an obviously fake smile. What did Cora know? Did she not want me meeting with her daughter? "I'm doing well. Yesterday, I took most of the day off to relax. I moved my whole life so quickly and hadn't taken time to adjust. It's like I only have one speed, but I'm learning to slow down."

"That's great, Allison. Ruby is in the back. She'll be out in a minute."

"Thanks."

"Can I get you anything? Lunch is on me, and as many cupcakes as you'd like."

How could Edison Carl Gardenia be married to such a delightful person as Cora? She was friendly and personable, willing to give me as many cupcakes as I wanted. Was it real? Perhaps it was a facade, and she was just as evil as he was. Maybe we all have a fake persona that we show the rest of the world, but inside we're a completely different person. I wouldn't be surprised if that were true. I had been putting on a mask my whole life. Dr. Baker tried to explain it away as depression. Perfectly hidden depression — the need for perfection and overachievement to mask our own insecurities or traumas. I wasn't saying Dr. Baker was wrong, be she was not right about everything.

"Well, if you gave me as many cupcakes as I wanted, I'd be as big as a house." I chuckled, showing off my light, playful mask. Hiding the mask that showed I was planning to study her and her family until I could prove her husband kidnapped and murdered my sister. She didn't need to know that. Nobody needed to know except Henry.

Ella being taken and the bar incident was the trauma tsunami in life that washed away the good-time friends while the real friends remained by my side in the storm's eye. Fun friends were nice to have, but the ride-or-dies were the ones who would help you bury the body or make it disappear without a trace. Not that I had been researching how to do that. Of course not. I wouldn't want that type of search associated with my IP address or hidden in my cookies. Not that I was planning to kill anybody, because I wasn't. Death would be too good for Edison Carl Gardenia. I wanted him to pay. Dearly.

"We start with one and then go from there," Cora said.

"Excellent idea. I'll have another of the s'more cupcakes to go with my green goddess salad."

"You got it."

Ruby emerged from the back room. I kept my composure, but her resemblance to Ella nearly took my breath away. "Hi, Ruby."

"Hi, Allison. Thank you so much for meeting with me."

"Any time."

As Cora plated my salad, she said, "Ruby, are you going to eat?"

"I'll grab a sandwich." She walked over to the cooler and grabbed a pre-made sandwich wrapped in cellophane. "Let's go over to the corner, so it's quieter."

Perfect. "Sounds great."

Cora called out that she would bring over my lunch. Ruby sat down, and I settled across from her. "So. Do you enjoy working here?"

"I do. It's nice to get out of the house," she said while she crumbled her napkin as if she were nervous.

"I know the feeling. I tend to be a hermit. But don't tell anybody; it's my big secret," I said, trying to make her feel at ease.

"Can I ask you a question?"

"Of course. What is it?"

She fidgeted with the cellophane wrap and unwrapped her sandwich before speaking. "The other day, when you were here, you ran out really fast. Was it something I did or said?"

I tried to soften my posture. "Oh no, not at all. I don't know if Liam explained, but you look so much like my sister that it startled me. It's nothing you did."

Ruby stared at me like she was looking right into my soul. "Oh. I, uh, just wanted to make sure I didn't offend you or something."

I was about to ask Ruby about her family when Cora approached with my salad. "Thank you."

"Enjoy. Now, I promise I'll be out of your hair."

"What were you about to say?"

"I was going to ask if you had any siblings."

She stared straight into my eyes for longer than was comfortable. It was unnerving.

"No, not really."

No, not really? What did that mean? "You're an only child?"

She nodded before taking a bite of her sandwich.

Was I imagining the strange reaction? How can you kind of be an only child? Unless she'd had a sibling who had died. After Ella, I remembered my mother struggling when someone would ask her how many children she had, and she had said two, but then changed her answer to one. Watching Ruby while I ate my salad, her likeness to Ella was indisputable, but there were definitely a few differences. Her chin was more pointed, and she didn't have Ella's freckles. Ella had freckles on the bridge of her nose that gave her that girl-next-door look that should be on the cover of magazines and billboards, modeling the latest fashion look.

She wasn't my Ella. I knew that because I was, in fact, rooted in reality. I knew I was sitting in front of Ruby Gardenia, a fourteen-year-old girl interested in software design.

She finished chewing. "So, you have a sister?"

"I do."

"Are you close?"

"We were. I haven't seen her in almost twenty years."

"Did you get into a fight?"

Shaking my head sadly, I said, "No, she was kidnapped when she was your age."

Her face fell. "Someone kidnapped your sister?"

"Yes, right in front of me."

"I'm so sorry. No wonder you bugged out when you saw me."

Bugged out. Ella used to say that. Shaking it off, I said, "It was surprising."

She set her hand atop mine. "I'm really sorry."

"Thank you. It's been a long time, and I'm learning to accept that she is gone and not coming back."

"Do you really believe that?"

"Sometimes."

Ruby nodded as if she understood. But how could she? Yet, there was something like an understanding between us.

"So, you're interested in software engineering?"

She took another bite of her sandwich and nodded. "Yeah, I've been homeschooled my whole life, and the computer and the internet have been my only access to the outside world. I'm curious about how it all works. I've been able to do some research on the topic, but my parents have a lot of controls on the computer, so I can't get too much information." She took another bite and finished chewing. "It's amazing how a little computer can connect people all around the world. It's crazy, right?"

"It is." Quite insightful for her age. Especially since she'd never been to public school. Cora must be smarter than I gave her credit for. Not that she seemed unintelligent, but she never gave off a brainy vibe. But she obviously knew a lot to have raised such a lovely young woman who was bright and friendly.

"Do you know what aspect of software engineering you'd like to learn, or are you just open to all things computers?"

"I'd like to know everything, but when Liam said you were a solutions architect, I was really, really interested in that. How did you get into it? What kind of stuff do you do? What exactly is a solutions architect?"

"Well, like you, computers always fascinated me. When I went to college, I took computer science and electrical engineering courses. I learned to write code to develop software applications like a website or program. But after a few years of working, I transitioned into the solutions architect field. A solutions architect creates the overall technical vision for a solution to a business problem. Like in finance, they will need a system for employees to submit expenses in a compliant way. That's a business problem. The solution will be the software application, or program, the employees will use to submit receipts and the details of the expenses. I work with a team to create the vision, or design, for it. I then manage the team that will develop and implement the system. And after all that's done, my team will continue to monitor and make updates to that system for the life of the program."

"Wow. So, you're kind of like a conductor in an orchestra but with computers."

"Kind of. Yeah."

"That's so cool. So, if I wanted to do something like that, I could start out as a developer and then become an architect?"

"Yes."

"Do you like your job?"

"I do. I enjoy working with people and creating something brand new." It was true. It was one reason I was drawn to the solutions architect role when the opportunity was presented to me. But all good things must come to an end. Or maybe I just needed a break. I could work with Henry for a while and then maybe go back to it.

"It sounds so cool. I would love to do that. What college did you go to?"

"I went to Caltech."

Ruby paused. "Did you grow up in California?"

"I did. In the Bay Area. A small town called Lafayette."

"Is Caltech near there?"

"No. Caltech is in southern California, about a six-hour drive. That was one reason I decided on the school — so that I could drive home if..."

"If your sister came back?"

This kid was killing me. It was like she could read the inside of me. "Yes, it was definitely one reason. I also want to stay close to my parents. They'd already lost one child. They had a really hard time with everything."

"I can only imagine."

"What are your parents like? Are you close?" I asked, trying to shift the conversation back to my goal, which was to find out more about the Gardenia family.

"Dad's okay, but he works a lot and well, you've met my mom."

"She seems great."

"Yeah, she is. So, were there a lot of girls in your college classes? I've read that there aren't a lot of female developers."

"Not very many, no. I'm not sure how it is now. There's probably a lot more than when I was an undergrad, but that didn't stop me. I'm not one to back down from a challenge." Not then, and certainly not now.

"That's cool. More boys to pick from, right?" she teased.

"Well, the odds were definitely in my favor."

We continued chatting casually. I learned that Ruby never had a boyfriend or a date. Her father was far too strict to allow it. When our time ended, I was disappointed and wished I didn't have a meeting to rush off to. I was enjoying my time with Ruby. She wasn't my sister, but it was like we had this connection I couldn't explain. Maybe it was because she reminded me of myself at her age. "I have a meeting to get to, which reminds me one major aspect of being a solutions architect is there are a lot of meetings. I'm in meetings almost all day... but I can show you a few things on my computer if you want to meet in my office next time. It's just down the street." I could also get her alone to ask more questions about her family. She might be holding back in front of Cora.

"That would be awesome, but I'll have to ask."

I stood up and slipped my messenger bag over my shoulder as I watched Ruby with her hands in the air, emphatically asking about coming to my office to learn more about computer architecture. Cora hesitated at first but then agreed. Perfect. The plan was going swimmingly.

TWENTY-FIVE

CORA

I COULDN'T SAY no to Ruby. Although I knew I had to ensure that Edison never, ever found out that I let her out of my sight, or there would be consequences. I had no doubt about that. The lunch seemed innocent enough. From what I could see, they were having a good time. On more than one occasion, I caught sight of smiles and laughter from the two of them. There wasn't anything to worry about. Ruby didn't know the truth, so it wasn't like she could tell Allison anything we didn't want her to know. But then again, if Ruby described details about our home to Allison, she may become suspicious. She, of course, would have no proof, so we'd probably be okay. But if Allison started poking around, it could reveal that I had let Ruby out on her own, and that could be terrible for all of us.

When the shop quieted down, I said, "Ruby, we need to talk about something."

"What is it?"

"I agreed to let you go to Allison's office, but you know not to tell your father that you're going, right?"

"Of course. He would totally bug out."

She was such a teenager. "Yes, he would. And you know not to tell her anything you shouldn't?"

"Like what?"

It was a good question. My paranoia was getting the better of me. There were things we didn't want Ruby to know, and certainly not Allison. "Well, you know how private your dad can be. Maybe avoid talking about Dad and our lives."

"Don't worry about it. I'm just learning about computers. That's all."

If that were true, I had nothing to worry about. We had never disclosed to Ruby the truth about our situation and figured since the lies we told were all she'd ever known, she wouldn't question it. But she was a clever girl. And I feared she may one day figure it out. Or had that day already come? If she'd known, she never acted like she did.

Ruby had never gone off on her own before. She'd always been with Edison, Dorothy, or me. Soon, I'd learn how trustworthy a fourteen-year-old could be. Not that she was running off to a club or to a concert in New York City. She was going to meet with her cousin's friend to talk about computers. It didn't get more innocent than that.

I hoped.

"Good."

"Don't even worry about it. Plus, she's Liam's girlfriend. She's practically family."

I didn't think she was his girlfriend. But I knew Liam wanted her to be. "I don't think they have that title yet."

"Well, then I'll put in a good word for him. Although I don't really know much about him."

It was a valid point. Ruby had only just met her cousin. For all she knew, he was a pedophile who trolled websites looking for young girls or some kind of psycho killer. But even though Liam had his rough spots in his younger years, he turned out to be a respectable young man. Well, I suppose he wasn't as young anymore at thirty-eight years old. "He's an amiable man."

"How come I haven't met him until recently?"

Ruby was perceptive, and I appreciated it at times, but other times, it made me nervous. "Well, we live in Seattle, and they were in Los Angeles. Plus, his mother, my sister, and I didn't always get along. But I spoke with her before he moved up here, and she says he's really turned things around, and now he's got a great job."

My sister, Patricia, hadn't approved of Edison, and it had caused a rift between us. Leaving us to only speak a few times a year by telephone. I hadn't seen her in years. Twenty years, to be exact. She was seven years older but thought she was a hundred years wiser. Patricia thought Edison was no good and that one day he'd be the death of me. I should have listened.

"What was Liam like before?" she said, her eyes narrowed.

"Oh, he was easily influenced by some unsavory elements when he was young and got into some trouble. Nothing serious. But that wasn't who he really was. I think who he is now is his true self. Studious, smart, dependable, good worker, and friendly."

"What did he do?"

"I don't think he'd appreciate me sharing his dirty laundry. But you can ask him about it if you'd like."

She shook her head. "Nah. I'm sure Allison's an excellent judge of character."

There was something about the way Ruby said that that brought the worried feeling back inside of me. I tried to shake it off because I'd seen her with Ruby. She seemed completely normal. No longer suspicious or wanting to know more about Edison and his activities. Sure, she'd acted weird when she met Ruby, but now it was like it had never happened. Liam explained she was on medication for some disorders relating to her past but that she was fine now. Maybe she was. Or maybe she wasn't and I was in for a rude awakening. "Yes, I'm sure she is."

Satisfied by my answers, Ruby scurried to the back. After a lesson in the kitchen the day before, I let her whip up a batch of strawberry lemonade cupcakes on her own. She was a quick learner. I was going to miss her when she went off to college. Or when our lives imploded and she hated me forever.

TWENTY-SIX

I DIDN'T FEEL like going out, but when Liam asked if I wanted to grab dinner, I realized I shouldn't turn him down. Despite my uneasiness around him, and lack of trust, he could have valuable information that could reveal Edison Carl Gardenia for what he really was — a monster. It was just something I had to do to ensure justice was served for Ella and whoever else Edison had harmed over the years. Not only that, but we worked together. That was something I hadn't thought completely through. When I first agreed to go out with Liam, I hadn't considered what would happen if it didn't end well. Awkwardness in the office wasn't a complication I needed. Although, if my plan worked, I would likely leave Seattle, and it wouldn't matter. Until then, I'd play nice with Liam and try to get all I could out of the relationship. At least he was easy on the eyes. And if he hadn't been related to Edison, maybe we could have been something. Pushing out the sad thought, I focused. Which was exactly why, after dinner, and acting completely normal and not psychotic — *Thank you very much, Dr. Baker* — I invited him back to my place for a nightcap. Of course, I would probably have tea, but he could have whatever liquor I had in the house, which once I thought about it, was only a bottle or two of wine that was still boxed in the garage.

But I didn't think Liam was dense enough to think that I wasn't inviting him back for a specific purpose that had nothing to do with alcoholic beverages. The more relaxed, the more open I could get him, the more I could learn from him. Like, for example, could I trust him? Did he know his uncle was a monster? Was Liam a monster?

Not only that, but I had formed a bond with Ruby, and I had a feeling she'd give me the information I needed, or at least something to prove Edison was no good. If I dumped her cousin, would Cora still let her meet with me? I couldn't risk it. The best plan was to get closer.

When I invited Liam back to my house, he seemed a bit surprised at first, but then the surprise turned to eagerness. And, hey, between you and me, I hadn't been romantic with anybody in quite some time. And like I said, Liam was adorable, with his dimples and sparkling, light brown eyes. I just hoped he wasn't a monster like the rest of his family. Although Ruby seemed delightful, and so did Cora. I had no reason to believe Cora was involved in Edison's evil, but I didn't have any evidence saying she wasn't either.

Based on what Ruby told me, Edison was controlling and very protective, which meant he could easily keep them under his thumb. An abuser didn't have to inflict visible bruises to be an abuser. There were plenty of abusers who controlled their victims without having to raise a single finger. The mere threat of the punishment and degradation of their sense of self, over time, was enough to scare them into obedience. And now that I thought about it, until the last few months when Cora opened her bakery and the sudden allowance of Ruby to attend school, a lot of the classic signs of coercive control were there. Isolation.

Monitoring activities during the day. Denying freedom and autonomy, like going to work or school. Limiting access to money. Reinforcing traditional gender roles. And those were just the signs I saw. An outsider who met them less than three weeks ago. If it were true, Cora had to know what Edison was capable of and maybe had even been forced to help abduct Ella. Knowing what he'd done to a young girl was likely enough to keep her scared and under his control. Would I be able to break Cora and get her to talk to me? Why hadn't I thought of that before? Because it was risky. Ruby and Liam were a better bet.

I arrived at my house before Liam but only by a few seconds. Driving into my garage, I noticed the light hadn't turned on. The lightbulb must've burned out. I shut off the engine and turned on the flashlight app on my phone. I didn't remember the light being out yesterday. Out of my car, I made my way inside the house, disarmed the security system, and then locked the garage door behind me. It was supposed to be a safe neighborhood, but you never know. *After all, my sister's kidnapper lives two doors down.*

Flipping the light switch on, I entered, slowing to evaluate if anything had been disturbed or if there was anyone lying in wait. Unlikely, considering the alarm seemed undisturbed. Reaching the kitchen, I saw nothing out of place. After a quick search of the upstairs, I was pretty sure the house was secure. I hurried to the front door and opened it. The porch light went on as expected. Maybe the garage light simply burned out. It happened. Liam was already parked and walking up the steps. "You made it," I said with a smile.

"It wasn't too tricky."

I had been the perfect date all evening. I laughed at his jokes and touched his arm. Like I wasn't hunting a killer. Thankfully, Liam and I had a lot in common. Since we were in the same field, we easily exchanged stories about projects and coworkers we had in common. Even some people we went to college with. To no surprise, he didn't know Henry. The thought of Henry made me think about whether he would find any dirt on Liam. "Come on in."

He stepped inside, and I locked the door. No need to arm the system since Liam was there. Either that was a mistake or a good thing. As he walked inside, he glanced over at my fireplace mantle. The one that had the photo of Ella and me. He had the same strange look on his face as the first time, but this time without surprise. "When you saw Ella's picture before, I'm surprised you didn't mention how much your cousin Ruby looks like her," I said, hopefully in a light tone. Really, I wanted to rip him a new one about it.

"There's certainly a resemblance, but I could tell they were different. And I wasn't sure if it would upset you or not."

So, let me meet her face-to-face without warning? My blood was heating, but I knew better than to push. "I wasn't upset, just surprised. It's surprising to see anybody look so much like her. I mean, I've now had lunch with Ruby, so I definitely see the differences in their appearance, but there is a striking resemblance."

Liam nodded apprehensively. "It's true."

The conversation halted. To turn it around, I said, "I'm pretty sure I have a bottle of wine or two, but it's in the garage."

"I'm surprised you haven't completely unpacked everything."

"To be honest, I was saving myself from it. I don't drink very often, so I figured it was best to leave it in the garage until I had a guest over, and now I have a guest over." I grinned, hoping he bought every single word.

"We don't have to have wine," he said brightly. As if he was handling me.

"Do you like tea?"

"I do."

I kept forgetting I'd spilled my dirty secrets to him the first time we hung out. He knew that the last time I drank too much, I'd attacked a man. He probably also knew liquor lowers one's inhibitions. So, he wasn't trying to take advantage of me or kill me. I hoped. The jury was still out on Liam, but that was one mark in his not-a-terrible-person column. "I have peppermint, chamomile, green peach, and ginger."

"Peppermint sounds good."

"Excellent choice. I'll put the kettle on," I said in a singsong voice and headed toward the kitchen. He followed close behind. I filled up the water in the kettle and set it back on its platform and pressed start.

Liam leaned against the counter, and I figured it was as good a time as any to make my move. I walked in front of him, and he put his hands on my waistline. He whispered, "Hi."

I said, "Hi," and placed my hands on his shoulders and brought my lips to his. They were soft and warm, and for a moment, I couldn't believe Liam was anything but good. As if an alarm bell went off, a loud set of knocks coming from the front door sounded through my house. Startled, I pulled back.

"Are you expecting anyone?" Liam asked.

Frozen in place, I said, "No."

The pounding started again, and my heart beat faster and faster. I hurried to the front door and looked out the peephole. It was the police. What were the police doing here? I opened the door. "Hello. Can I help you with something?"

"Are you Allison Smythe?"

They were there for me? "Yes."

"Ma'am, we received a call from a Dr. Virginia Baker. She was concerned for your safety and requested a welfare check on you. She said she hadn't heard from you in a few days, and that wasn't usual."

My cheeks burned with embarrassment. I glanced over at Liam, trying to conceal my rage toward Dr. Baker. "I assure you, I'm perfectly fine. This is a friend and coworker, Liam Parker, and we were just about to have a cup of tea. Would you like to come in and have a cup? The kettle's still on."

"That's kind of you, but if you don't mind, we'd like to come in and look around?"

"Sure. Please come in."

The officers nodded as they entered the house and requested both of our identification before conducting their search.

Seething, I turned to Liam and calmly said, "My therapist sent them. She wanted me to call her every day, but I told her I would only meet with her once a week. I've been ignoring her calls since she wouldn't take no for an answer."

"Are you sure that is a good idea?" he asked.

"Yes, I'm sure. I don't need a babysitter."

Liam and I stood there in silence as I thought of all the ways I wanted to tell off Dr. Baker, starting with ending our relationship. It was no longer court ordered, and I could be a free person if I wanted to be. Although I needed to keep my meds. Well, I would keep her until I could find a different therapist, one who didn't think I was a psycho.

After a few minutes, the officers returned. "Looks like everything is in order. And you're sure you're okay?"

"I am more than okay. Dr. Baker is my therapist. She's been worried about me since I moved here by myself. I haven't been answering her calls, so I guess she thought something was wrong, even though I repeatedly told her I would speak with her at our scheduled weekly meeting."

"All right, ma'am, you have a good night. You too, sir."

The two officers left, and I shut the door. Liam said from behind, "Maybe you should call your therapist and get this sorted out."

"You're right, I should."

"Maybe I should go."

Now I was really going to give Dr. Baker a piece of my mind. "It is getting late."

We stood there awkwardly, staring at each other for a moment longer than I could take. "I'll see you at work?"

"Yes, of course."

There was no goodbye kiss. Of all the first and last kisses, that was by far the most maddening.

Now it was time for me to give Dr. Baker a piece of my mind. She had no right to do this. Yes, I'd avoided her texts and voicemails, but only after I firmly stated in the text after our last session that I was only willing to meet on Mondays from now on. She had no right to send the police to my house. She had no evidence that I was a psychotic person or had a psychotic disorder. Where did she get off? If I was psychotic, then she should be very worried, but luckily, I wasn't. So, all she was going to receive was a verbal lashing. Or not. That might make me seem crazy. I pulled out my phone and texted her.

> I'm fine. Please don't send the police to my house again.

We could talk on Monday at our scheduled time, and I would tell her rationally, not being hotheaded or angry, that I didn't appreciate her interrupting my date with a visit from the police.

TWENTY-SEVEN

Sitting across from my sister's teenage lookalike, I realized I had more than one reason to be meeting with Ruby. It was a pleasant distraction while I waited for more information from Henry. And computers were easy to get lost in. Ruby genuinely seemed to want to learn all about my world. Where I grew up. What it was like to have a sister. What it was like to be an engineer. What it was like to work for a big corporation like Troodle. She seemed to want to take it all in. She was wide-eyed and ready to take on the universe.

She was smart and ambitious, like I had been at her age. But there was something about her that made me think we were more alike than I originally thought. It wasn't just our shared interest in computers, but her mannerisms and the fact I could tell she was holding back information from me. I also sensed part of her sunny disposition was an act, perhaps because of her controlling father. Or a secret she was hiding. Like Edison had taken her too, and the details of her life were a lie. It was the only logical explanation for why she looked so much like Ella. Edison had a type. And after he was done with my sister, he took her as a replacement. Ruby was probably not the first after Ella. If I was right, he may take another and another. Edison needed to be stopped.

I wanted to be a person for Ruby to confide in. To tell her truth to. I would protect her and make sure she would get through this. It would be tough for a teen to stand up against her abuser. Maybe Ruby sensed it too, because I could tell she was in for something more than just a career mentor. She wanted the connection to the rest of the world, and I really wanted to give it to her. I wanted her to go home to her family and save that family from what mine had gone through.

I pointed the screen at one of the architectural components. "Right there. That's where it happens."

She nodded. "It's so cool."

I turned to her and said, "You know, if you ever need someone to talk to about anything, not just computers or college, I'm here."

She chewed on her fingernail, and a zing went through my body. Ella used to chew her nails when she was nervous. *Ruby is not Ella.*

"What is it?"

"I'm curious about your sister. What was she like? You said that she was my age when she was kidnapped."

Did she know Edison was my sister's kidnapper? Or at least suspected it? Maybe he had told her stories about how she wasn't the first or the second or the third. The more I thought about it, the more it made sense. I said, "Ella was like sunshine. She was creative and always in a good mood. Of course, unless we were fighting over clothes, which I admit happened a lot. She loved music and painting. For my sixteenth birthday, she painted a picture of the two of us. And mind you, at the time, I was sixteen, and she was only thirteen. She was very talented, but she was still working on her craft. In the painting, we looked distorted, almost like a Picasso or something Picasso's child would make. She handed it to me, and I was so touched, but I couldn't help but laugh. She laughed too and said, 'Don't worry, that's not what you really look like.' Ella had such a good sense of humor," I said, with a sad smile as I thought about the *before* times.

"So, she was an optimistic person. Someone who didn't let things get her down."

"Yeah. She was definitely a glass-half-full type, you know, like always saw the potential for good instead of bad."

"Were you two alike when you were young?"

I chuckled. "Oh no, we were opposites. Ella was the outgoing cheerleader dance team artist. I was more the academic and saw in black and white. Ella's world was filled with color."

"But you got along. Like best friends?"

"Yeah, other than her stealing my clothes. We were absolutely best friends. Always." I bit my lip and tried to force the tears to stop.

"I'm so sorry they took her from you."

I grabbed a tissue and dabbed my eyes. "It's not something you ever get over."

Ruby looked into my eyes and said, "I have a secret."

"You do?"

She nodded. "Yes. Will you promise not to tell anybody?"

For now. "I pinky swear." I held up my pinky finger, and we linked. "I swear."

I thought this was it. I was going to learn the truth. With my heart pounding, I waited.

Ruby said, "Cora is not my mother."

I knew it. "What do you mean she's not your mother?"

"When I was little, like really little, they told me she was my mother, and she took care of me. They think I remember nothing before that. But I do. And I can't wait to go to college to get away from her and from him."

For the first time, I saw fury in Ruby's eyes. Cora was as bad as Edison. Or she was under his control. I was unsure which it was, but I knew Cora couldn't be trusted.

Little doubt had remained about Edison Carl Gardenia's character, but now there was none. There was zero doubt that he took my sister, and it sounded like he took Ruby, too. The puzzle was complete. Pedophiles have a type. And Edison's was little girls with strawberry blonde hair, blue eyes, and peaches and cream complexions. Keeping calm, I asked, "Ruby, are you safe?"

She nodded. "You don't have to worry about me, but I thought since you shared with me, I would share with you."

"Are you sure? If you're not, I can protect you. We can go to the police. You won't be in any trouble."

"I promise. I'm okay."

Had she developed Stockholm syndrome? Why didn't she want to go to the police? He must have taken her. Why was she protecting him?

I'd stay close to her. When she was ready, we'd expose him.

Ruby eyed me cautiously. "You said I look like your sister. Do you have a picture?"

Maybe she was also trying to gather evidence? "Not here."

"I'd like to see a picture of her. Would you show me next time?"

I wished she would tell me more, but I didn't want to push too hard. I could be a little patient. If I tried. "Yes, I can do that."

"Cool. Thanks, Allison."

Our meeting ended on a somber tone, but I waved goodbye with a smile as she left and went back to the bakery. I hadn't expected to get so much information so quickly. I wondered if I should tell Detective White that Edison likely took Ruby too. What was Ruby's real name? It sounded like they took her when she was really young. Was her family still looking for her? I would discover the truth about Edison Carl Gardenia, and Cora and Ruby, and what he had done with my sister.

Edison would never see it coming.

TWENTY-EIGHT

WALKING IN TO MY OFFICE, I laughed as Ruby joked about living on a diet of cupcakes and how she would adjust the flavors to ensure all the food groups were covered. She was clever and creative and didn't seem traumatized at all. Maybe that was because they took her when she was so young? Maybe Cora had cared for her. It seemed like Cora adored Ruby. Maybe that was why? I said, "A solid plan," as I shut the door behind me. Ruby picked up the visitor chair and set it next to mine. We had an important meeting today.

After long deliberation and watching the comings and goings of the Gardenia house over the weekend, I decided I needed to ask Ruby more about her situation. I needed to know, for sure, if they had kidnapped her like Ella had been. In my surveillance, I had spotted nothing unusual outside the Gardenia house and I had taken several walks, peered behind bushes, and watched as Edison drove off to Lord knows where while Cora and Ruby didn't leave the house all weekend. It made me sad that they never went anywhere. I was glad that, Monday through Friday, Ruby could go to the bakery with

Cora. Otherwise, from what I understood, she didn't really get out much at all except for the occasional trip to the grocery store or to get new clothes. But I didn't think that happened very often. I was more and more convinced Ruby was a victim of Edison. Just like Ella.

Seated behind my desk. I said, "I'm happy to keep meeting with you and discussing different career options and really anything you want to, but there's something that's been bothering me that I want to talk to you about."

Ruby's face paled. I could tell I had worried her, and that wasn't my intention. "It's not anything you've done. It's just some concerns I have about your home life."

"Like what?" She inched away from me.

"You said that Cora is not your biological mother."

"She's not. But they tell me I have to tell people that."

"Do you remember how I told you my sister was kidnapped at your age? Well, I started thinking maybe you were kidnapped, too. Do you remember if that happened?"

Ruby's body relaxed. Well, I guess I was wrong about that, but I was not wrong that something fishy was going on in the Gardenia household. "I wasn't kidnapped, I promise. It's just complicated."

"It's complicated?"

"I promise you my dad is my dad, but Cora is not my mom. From what I gathered, from conversations I overheard, Cora couldn't have children. And so when Dad had me with another woman, they decided I would be Cora and his baby and not the other woman's baby."

That didn't sound normal at all. Who was her mother? I was sure she didn't just hand her baby over to that monster and his wife. "Do you ever see or talk to your biological mother?"

Ruby swallowed again, looking nervous. "I'd rather not talk about it."

She still wasn't comfortable telling me everything. Had Edison killed her mother? It was par for the course for a person like him. But he didn't seem like someone who would go to that length for his wife. Unless he had a reason to get rid of the other woman.

"Are you happy in your situation?"

"Well, I wish things were different. I'd like more freedom and friends my age. My whole life, it's been just Dad and Cora and... For a long time, I thought what I had was enough, but meeting you and working at the bakery and knowing that I'm going to high school with other kids, I realize it's not enough. I just don't want anybody to get hurt."

Who would get hurt? Edison? I stared at this young woman, perplexed. I could tell she had another secret but didn't feel comfortable telling me or was afraid to tell me. "You know you can tell me anything, and I promise you won't get in to trouble."

"It's not that. I'm not sure yet."

I nodded but didn't understand what she wasn't sure about. "Take your time. I just want to help." I knew there was something strange going on in the Gardenia residence. Dr. Baker said I was crazy and wanted to lock me up and have me evaluated. *I don't think so.* No, I was right about this.

Ruby said, "Speaking of family, did you bring a picture of your sister?"

"I did." I opened my drawer and pulled out the envelope I had brought from home. I slid the photo out. It was a picture of Ella and me a few months before they kidnapped her. We wore matching smiles, and I had an arm around Ella's shoulder. Dad had taken the photo. We had been goofing off in the back yard when he said he wanted to preserve the moment. We told him he was corny, but he waved us off before running into the house to get his camera. I wondered if he knew in his heart we only had a few more months with Ella. Father's intuition or some-thing. He came back out to the yard, and we did a series of poses for him. He said this picture was his favorite because we looked natural and happy and we were being goofy and silly, like we acted most of the time. In some ways, it was a memory of my dad and of Ella. They were wonderful memories, and even if I never saw my sister again, at least I had that. I handed the picture to Ruby. "That's Ella on the left, and that's me next to her. Can you see the resemblance between the two of you?"

Her eyes fixated on Ella's photo, and she didn't respond. Ruby's reaction to the photo of Ella was a lot like mine when I saw Ruby at the bakery the first time. It was one of those moments when you had to pause and check that your brain was working correctly. Probably a full minute later, she said, "Can I keep this?"

"Oh." I hadn't expected that she would want to keep a photo of us.

Before I could answer, she said, "Can I borrow it? Just for a little bit. I'll give it back, I promise."

"Okay. Let me just take a picture of it real quick with my phone." I picked up my phone and snapped a photo. I had been meaning to do it, anyway. There were companies that would take all of your printed photos and digitize them. That way, they would never get destroyed in a fire or lost in a move. They could then store the photos in the cloud forever unless, of course, there was a digital apocalypse.

She looked at it and then at me. "Don't worry. I'll give it back."

"Okay." I wondered why she wanted to keep it. Ruby certainly had her own secrets she wasn't sharing with me. I wondered if maybe she knew something about Ella. Like she'd seen photos of her. Maybe Edison had taken photographic evidence of his crimes against my sister. The thought made my stomach flip and flop.

"You were going to show me the architecture design that your team came up with last week. Can I see it?"

She was clever and knew to change the conversation because of how strange all of this was. What was Ruby hiding? "Yes, of course." I inched closer to my desk and pulled up the latest schematic that my team had created. As I pointed out the different components in the diagram, I tried to direct attention to her life once again. "Do you have any friends or neighbors you hang out with?"

"Uh, not really." She said apprehensively before returning her attention to the screen. I guess that's all she had to say about that. Ruby was not your typical teenager, but she tried to be. I had a feeling her exterior wall was even thicker than my own. Perhaps Ruby suffered from depression and didn't even know it, or she had evil in her like her father did. But I had a hard time believing that, even though I didn't know her very well.

Over the weekend, I didn't see her go anywhere. From what I understood, Cora and Ruby didn't go anywhere or do anything without Edison's approval. I only hoped Ruby opened up to me, and soon, because I wanted to make sure she was safe once we took Edison down.

TWENTY-NINE

After my last meeting with Ruby, there was no question she knew more about Ella than she was telling me. Thoughts about the Gardenia house whirled and swirled in my mind. I needed to get closer. I needed to get inside and get proof. The way she looked at the photo of Ella and me made me think she'd seen us before, or at least Ella. Something triggered a memory in her, but she guarded that secret. Why? I didn't want to scare Ruby off, so it was up to me to figure it out on my own.

One thing I had discovered when researching predators was that serial killers and other criminals had a tendency to keep trophies. Maybe he'd kept something of Ella's after he did whatever he did with her. Or took photos of her when he had her. That would explain how Ruby had seen Ella's face before.

No longer concerned with my workplace attendance, I sent a message to my team that I had a doctor's appointment and would work from home. It wasn't true, but they didn't need to know that. Dressed in a pair of black joggers, a black hoodie, black gloves, and brand-new black tennis shoes, I was ready for what came next. It was the only way.

I wouldn't typically break in to a house and search for evidence of a kidnapping or murder, but these weren't normal times. And this was certainly not something I would discuss with Dr. Baker. If she knew, she'd bring those cops back to my house for sure. I still didn't understand why she thought I was suddenly crazy. If I were crazy when she met me five years ago, I wouldn't be so bothered. Heck, I had thought I'd gone crazy. But this was five years later. I still couldn't believe she'd sent the police to my house. That's all I needed was someone watching me all the time.

I could feel it in my bones. I was close to exposing Edison Carl Gardenia and freeing Ruby from the life of seclusion that he'd forced on her. He needed to be stopped.

Gloved up, I shut the front door of my house and casually strolled down my driveway, heading toward the Gardenia house. Based on my surveillance over the weekend, the house didn't appear to have any cameras, so I didn't think I'd be caught. When I reached the Gardenia driveway, I turned around and surveyed the neighborhood. No cars were driving by, and no one was out on their lawn or in their driveway. I didn't see anyone and hopefully nobody saw me. But if they did, I would say that I was there to visit Ruby or drop off a message for her.

From what I could tell, there was a side door that went into the garage with a layout similar to my house. I figured that would be my best bet to get inside. Most people didn't lock the interior of the garage that went into the house.

Sure the coast was clear, I ran down the side of the house and reached the garage. From the pocket of my hoodie, I pulled out a flashlight. It wasn't dark outside, but I wanted something heavy to potentially break the window to get in or to use as a weapon in case I encountered trouble. Like Edison coming home unexpectedly. I jiggled the door handle, but it didn't budge. It was unusually quiet outside, and I hoped breaking the window wouldn't startle a neighbor or alert a neighborhood dog.

Quickly, I gave up on the plan and rushed over to the other side of the house. Sweat dripped down my back as I found all the other windows were locked, too. After a scan of the neighborhood, I ran back over to the garage door. With the end of the flashlight, I whacked the corner of the window and jumped back. The break was loud but effective. I crouched down and peered up, trying to hear a dog or anything that showed someone had heard me. But the neighborhood remained silent. It was the middle of the day. There weren't a lot of kids in the neighborhood, so none were in the streets playing. Most people were at work. I covered my hand with my sleeve and reached through the broken glass to unlock the door. I quietly opened the door and shut it behind me, realizing any noise at this point wasn't an issue.

The garage had cabinets and racks filled with boxes. Was this where he kept his mementos? I opened the cabinets only to find canned goods and other household products like paper towels, toilet paper, that kind of thing. Over in the racks were cardboard boxes. They were labeled with different names of the family members: Cora, Ruby, and Edison. I slid the box labeled "Edison" off the bottom shelf and opened the flaps. Thumbing through the contents, I found old clothing. Nothing more. I repeated with a second and found more winter clothes. Wondering if the box labels were meant to throw people off, I went through Cora and Ruby's too but again found nothing but old clothing. There were tools hanging from the wall and a bench with drawers and cabinets below. It was one of the most organized garages I had ever seen. Opening the cabinets, I discovered solvents, cleaners, oils, and nothing you wouldn't expect to find in a garage. Rustling through the drawers, I found nothing that led me to Ella. Best case, I could poke around in the garage and find what I needed. But that wasn't the situation. I had to go inside the house.

At the door to the house, I turned the knob and lucked out. I stepped inside and was instantly filled with an eeriness, like I'd entered another dimension. I had never gone into some-body's house without them. It was such a violation, but it was necessary in this case.

The house was as tidy as the garage. Immaculate was prob-ably a better word. It was typical for an abuser to require his victims to keep a shipshape home. Cora had probably got the brunt of his attitude, maybe even his fists.

Creeping down the hallway, I noticed there weren't any family photos on the walls. Odd. Reaching the kitchen, I deduced it hadn't been updated since the nineteen nineties, but it was clean. The dining room had a credenza with drawers. I wouldn't think that would be where he would keep any mementos, but I was there, and it was my one opportunity to know for sure. I creaked open the drawers, but they were filled with nothing but napkin holders, cloth napkins, and typical household items. Searching through the rest of the drawers, I found nothing out of the ordinary.

Behind me, the window shaded. I turned around, but there was nothing there. Maybe my mind was playing tricks on me. The hairs on the back of my neck prickled. Surely, it was just nerves. Out of luck in the kitchen and dining room, I went into the living room, but there really wasn't anywhere to hide anything. No drawers, just a TV stand, fireplace, and mantle. The layout was a lot like my house.

On the mantle were a few pictures of Edison, one of Cora, and one young photo of Ruby. That was it. None of the pictures were of them together, which was strange. It almost looked like they staged it to make it look like people lived there.

I headed toward the stairs and took one step, then another. When the staircase creaked, my heart nearly beat out of my chest. Freaked out, I turned around, expecting to see someone behind me, but there was no one. After that, I hurried up the stairs. The first door on the right looked like it was Ruby's bedroom, with its pink bedspread and white iron bed frame, a desk, and closet. There weren't rockstar posters on the walls, but there were drawings and watercolor paintings. Ruby was a pretty talented artist. It surprised me she hadn't mentioned it. I opened and closed her drawers and saw nothing related to Ella, so I continued to the next room that appeared to be Cora and Edison's bedroom. I rifled through the walk-in closet but found nothing of interest. Over at the dresser, I opened the top drawer to find socks and boxer shorts. Obviously, Edison's. Thankfully, I was wearing gloves. I didn't want to touch anything of his with my bare fingers.

Despite my rummaging, I saw nothing related to Ella. Nothing that would give me a clue to what happened to her. This house was like mine, which meant I had one more room to check. Sure enough, down the hall, I found what looked like a study. There was a large oak desk, an executive chair, and a bookshelf filled with books. I stepped closer to inspect the titles. Mostly classics, probably for show. I stood behind his desk and was about to open the top drawer when the clink of a rock hitting the window startled me.

How could a rock hit the second-floor window? Was it a bird? With my heart racing, I watched as another hit the window. It wasn't a bird. Standing as still as I could, I listened. The sound of a car engine grew nearer and nearer. I had to get out of there.

Why were they home already? I ran out of the room and down the stairs and headed back toward the garage but realized that was where they parked their cars. I rushed back to the slider, through the kitchen, and ran out into the back yard. There was no sign pointing to the origin of the rocks, but I wasn't looking too hard. Breathing heavily, I reached the back gate, flipped open the latch, and ran and hid until I heard the opening and close of the garage door. Once shut, I crept down until I was sure nobody would spot me.

Once I hit the road, I sprinted back to my house and pushed my way inside, locking the door and setting the alarm before sliding down to the floor. With labored breathing, I leaned against my front door and wondered why they came home early and who or what had been warning me to get out of there. I had seen no signs of another person. Maybe I had imagined it.

A buzzing in my pocket made me nearly jump out of my skin. I pulled out my phone and read a text from Liam.

Hey, I heard you're WFH. Everything okay?

I thought, *maybe, maybe not.*

THIRTY

CORA

RUBY and I were singing along to the radio when I approached the house. The sight in front of our home startled me, and I slammed on the brakes. It felt like someone had knocked the wind out of me. I wasn't sure if it was the seatbelt or the fear gripping my insides. Was it time? Had someone found us out? "Why are there police cars here?" Ruby asked.

That was exactly what I was wondering. Maybe it wasn't time. Maybe something happened to Edison. Were we that lucky?

With my pulse racing, I pulled the car over and parked on the road before rushing toward the front door. Ruby pattered behind me. The door was unlocked. I stepped inside and spotted Edison standing with two police officers. His face was beet-red, obviously outraged. I knew the look. I knew the rage. Edison said to the two officers, "This is my wife Cora and our daughter Ruby."

"What happened?" I asked frantically.

"Somebody broke in."

Thieves? "When did this happen?"

"About an hour ago. The police think they left right before I came in. They broke the window on the side door of the garage and let themselves in. But they didn't leave through the garage, at least not when I was here. The back slider was open. So, they likely left through the back yard."

The back yard. Had Edison checked the back yard before the police arrived? Why had he called the police? Was he so sure we'd never be caught? "Did they take anything?"

The younger of the two officers said, "Ma'am, we're not sure. We need you and your daughter to look and see if anything is missing. Your husband said that he found nothing out of place."

That would be strange, wouldn't it? "They broke in, but they didn't take anything?"

The same officer said, "We think your husband interrupted the burglary. They had to get out fast and didn't have time to take anything. But we'll still need you to look and check if anything is missing."

I nodded. "We'll check now."

Edison said, "Yes, go now."

My heart beat faster as I ran up the stairs to check our bedroom. I was sure Edison had already done so. I could only imagine the mood he would be in after the police officers left. Who would break into our home? Why our house of all houses? We kept a tidy home. It wasn't extravagant. We didn't have expensive cars or anything to make a burglar think we had something of value to take. It didn't make any sense.

Nothing was missing from my wardrobe or drawers. I had little jewelry other than my wedding ring and a necklace that Edison had given me on our one-year wedding anniversary. It was the only jewelry he had ever given me. I walked over to Ruby's room. "Anything missing?"

"No."

She had a strange look on her face. Maybe she was scared about somebody breaking into our home. What if we had been home? Were they violent? Would they have attacked us? Wouldn't that be something to have survived Edison only to be attacked and killed by a complete stranger? I walked up to Ruby and put my arm around her. "We're going to be okay. I'll talk to Daddy about putting in a security system to make sure this doesn't happen again."

Ruby just stared ahead and nodded. The poor thing was terrified.

"Let's go back downstairs and talk to Daddy, okay?" Without a word, Ruby followed me down the stairs and into the kitchen, where the police officers stood near the dining table as he took notes on his clipboard. I declared, "Nothing is missing."

"Sounds like you folks got lucky and scared off the perp, and he didn't have time to take anything of value."

I glanced at the glass slider. "They went out there?"

"It was open when I came inside. They had to have."

In the thirty years we had lived there, I had seen no criminal activity in our neighborhood. These were hard times we were living in. Maybe the criminals finally came to our little piece of Seattle. It was time for a security system.

After the police officers wrapped up, we thanked them and shut the door behind them.

Edison commanded. "Ruby, go to your room now."

She hurried up the stairs without a fuss.

"I think we should get a security system, Edison."

"Oh you do, do you?"

I said, "I do," as I backed away from him.

With the devil in his eyes, he said, "Well, if you didn't have your little bakery, you would have been home, and the burglar wouldn't have let themselves in, thinking they could take whatever they wanted. This is your fault. Don't you think?"

"I don't know." It figured he would find a way to blame me for this. Everything was always everybody else's fault. Never Edison's. He clenched his fists. Edison didn't hit me often, but I knew he was capable of it. He was capable of horrible things.

I shrank into myself and said, "I'll ask Dorothy if she saw anything."

"You do that. And know that if this ever happens again, you will shut down the bakery."

"Okay, that's fair, but I think maybe we should get a security system, anyhow?"

"I'll take care of it. Go ask the pet if she saw anything."

A shiver ran down my spine. Such a grotesque nickname. The pet. The neighbor. I maneuvered around Edison, headed toward the back door, and made my way out to the back yard.

On the far edge of our property, I approached the small studio and knocked on the door. Dorothy opened up right away. "Hi, Cora. What's up? Is it time for dinner?"

"No, we had a break-in earlier today, and Edison wanted me to ask if you saw anything."

"No, nothing," she said, seemingly unperturbed by the fact that we had a break-in.

"Are you sure? They ran out the back. Well, that's what the police think, anyhow."

Dorothy cocked her head. "The police were here?"

"Yes, Edison called to make a police report."

She shook her head. "Well, I didn't see anything, so I probably can't be of any use."

"And you didn't hear anything, either?"

"I don't think so."

"They broke the window on the side door to the garage. It must've been loud."

Dorothy shrugged. "What time was it? I was probably watching TV and didn't hear it."

"It was around three o'clock."

"Yeah, I was watching TV. Sorry. If I see anything, I'll let you know, and I'll keep a lookout. Don't worry, I'll lock my door," she said with a weak smile.

I never really trusted Dorothy, and if you asked me, I thought she was too calm about the situation. The sound of grass crunching behind me caught my attention. Turning, I said, "Oh, hi, Ruby."

"Hi. You didn't see anything?"

Dorothy shook her head again. "Nope, nothing," she said with very little emotion. I glanced down and noticed something in Dorothy's hand. A photograph. My eyes widened, and I wasn't sure my heart could take any more surprises today. "What is that?"

"What is what?"

"That thing you have in your hand."

"Oh, that's nothing."

I knew it was something. "Let me see it."

Dorothy lifted her hand, displaying a photo on her palm.

I felt like someone had kicked me in the chest. "Where did you get that?"

Ruby said, "I gave it to her."

I glanced at Ruby, who wore a devilish smirk. I stared back at the photo and fell to my knees. It was over. It was all over.

THIRTY-ONE

AT THIS POINT, I didn't care if I lost my job or not, so I emailed in that I would work from home for the rest of the week. Well, I cared a little. Okay, I cared a lot, but at that moment, all I could think about was the Gardenia house. The more I thought about the events of that afternoon, the more convinced I was that somebody had warned me to get out of the house. If I hadn't seen the second rock hit the window, I could have rationalized that it had been a bird accidentally pecking at the window. But I saw it. There was no bird.

Was it Ruby? Had she been home and was warning me that her parents were arriving any second? Was she trying to protect me? Why? The closer I thought I was to the truth, the more questions I had.

After finding nothing in the home, strangely, I was even more intrigued. Even with no physical evidence that Edison Carl Gardenia was the one who took my sister, it did not deter me. Because Henry's cryptic call explaining that he was driving up from the Bay Area told me he had something on Edison. This was it. It was going to be over soon.

Glancing at the clock on my monitor, I tapped the desk in anticipation of Henry's arrival. He'd texted an hour ago that he would be at my house any minute.

After tossing and turning all night, I had played nearly every scenario in my mind. Did Henry find surveillance footage? Flight receipts? Whatever it was would prove Edison and his accomplice had taken Ella. I was right, and I wasn't crazy.

My attempts at focusing on work failed miserably. Thankfully, most of my employees were pretty self-sufficient and needed little guidance. Only half listening in on the meetings I attended virtually, I realized I was finally one of those employees who barely put in the minimum effort when they were supposed to be working from home but were really taking care of a sick child or watching Netflix while downing cold medicine. I didn't enjoy being that person, but all I could think about was finding the truth about Ella and making sure Edison was brought to justice. He needed to tell us where she was so we could bring her home and bury her for real.

Mom and Dad had wanted to have a memorial for her. I had fought them vehemently, arguing that we didn't know she was dead and that she could be out there somewhere. In the end, I complied. I refused to cry at the service because I couldn't let myself believe she was gone. But it had been twenty years, and I no longer believed in fairy tales.

There was something in Edison's eyes that told me I'd never see Ella again, and he enjoyed knowing I knew. Sitting here, pretending to pay attention to a meeting, I realized that being so close to bringing Edison to justice meant I would soon learn the truth. No more speculation. And I didn't think it would be what I wanted so badly to hear.

The sound of Marvin's voice in the meeting reached me. "Allison, are you in agreement?"

I did not know what they were talking about. I quickly unmuted myself and said, "Yes, I agree."

The sound of Marvin's voice reminded me of our last conversation in my office. He told me to never give up. And I hadn't until now. But maybe he was right. I had to hang on to that hope for a little longer. Not knowing was so much worse than knowing. At least that's what I thought. If we got Edison to confess that he kidnapped and murdered Ella, would that be better? It wouldn't be any different for my mother, who'd accepted that Ella was gone forever. Maybe I just didn't want to believe the worst. Not that a belief could stop the worst from happening.

A knock on the door startled me. I left the meeting and jumped out of my chair and rushed to the door. After disarming the security system, I opened the door. "Henry, I'm glad to see you."

"You too. I need the bathroom."

"You know where it is."

Henry ran off with his backpack and messenger bag. Shutting the door and engaging the alarm, I couldn't wait to hear what he'd found. I had already hit the grocery store and bought all of Henry's favorite snacks. It was the very least I could do. He drove twelve hours for me — again.

My phone buzzed. I glanced at the screen. A text from Liam. I decided not to respond in case Henry came back. I wouldn't delay another moment if I didn't have to. Liam could wait. I moved myself to the kitchen and leaned against the counter, anxiously awaiting Henry's return. He walked in more relaxed than before. "Hi." I smiled wide and wrapped my arms around Henry, squeezing him tight. "Thank you! Thank you! Thank you!"

He stayed quiet as he gently pushed me back. "Well, let me show you what I have first before you triple thank me."

"Can I get you anything? Coffee? Candy?"

"Caffeine and sugar would be great."

I nodded, and he said, "I'll set up on the dining table."

The anticipation was nearly killing me, but it didn't stop me from pressing a button on the espresso maker. I should make one for myself, but then again, maybe I shouldn't. My nerves were already in overdrive, as if I had downed ten espresso shots.

Henry wouldn't have come back unless he had something good. The coffee brewed, and I grabbed the full cup and headed over to the pantry to grab the bags of Reese's Peanut Butter Cups and Sour Patch Kids. I wasn't sure what kind of mood he was in, chocolate or sugar or both. I set them down on the table along with the coffee.

Henry smiled. "The good stuff." He took a swig of the espresso before reaching for the Reese's Peanut Butter Cups. He pulled one out of the bag, unwrapped the foil, and popped it into his mouth. He chewed and chewed and then, after he swallowed, he said, "All right, let me show you what I found."

I sat in the chair next to him. We were nearly touching as I stared at his computer screen. "What am I looking at here, Henry?"

"This is a set of flight reservations from twenty years ago."

I didn't quite get the connection. My lack of understanding must have shown on my face. He continued, "You told me he travels a lot for work, so it took me a while to get into a bunch of old airline manifests. But I finally got some hits. Apparently, Gardenia is a fan, or was a fan, of United Airlines and is a preferred gold member. So, I started digging and looking for dates around when Ella disappeared." He scrolled the screen and then stopped and pointed to one line. "As you can see, it's two days before Ella disappeared, and it's a one-way ticket."

"How did he get back?" I asked, wide-eyed.

"That is the right question, my dear friend, Allison," he said with glee. He minimized the screen and pulled up another. "From there, I searched rental car records, with no luck. But then I checked DMV records for sales of white vans around that time." He pointed to the screen. "And look here. The day he landed at Oakland International Airport, he also purchased a white van."

A chill went down my spine. "The white van."

Henry nodded.

My nightmares had been filled with the white van and Edison Carl Gardenia grabbing my sister and throwing her in the back seat before hopping in. Stunned, I processed the information. It was the smoking gun. "And do you know where the van is now?"

"I thought you'd never ask." He popped up another window on his computer. "As you can see here, the van was decommissioned a year later. An accident. Some sort of fire."

To destroy evidence. This was all circumstantial. But this proved I wasn't crazy, and Edison Carl Gardenia took my sister. *Wait.* He wasn't alone. "Did anybody else fly down with him?"

Henry nodded. "His wife, Cora."

My mouth dropped open. Cora. Friendly, cupcake-baking Cora. Cora helped kidnap my sister. Perhaps she was just doing what Edison wanted. A woman under the control of her husband? That was the best-case scenario. The worst case was that she was as evil as her husband. And what about Liam? I turned to Henry. "I know Cora. We've chatted on several occasions."

Henry's eyes widened. "She's dangerous, and if she knows who you are, you're in danger."

"Did you find anything on Liam?"

He shook his head. "Nothing bad. Just some petty stuff in his youth. But I found that he was on a trip to Disneyland with his band when Ella was taken. So, he couldn't have been involved."

Liam was innocent. But could I forgive his family connections? I knew the answer. *No*.

We'd found him. *Them*. The monster and his wife.

Ruby had confided in me that Cora was not her mother. But she also said they had not kidnapped her. But now, I wondered if she was too afraid to tell me. Cora had a history, and so did Edison. Ruby was in danger. I scratched the back of my head, scrunching up my hair, trying to make sense of all of this. "Henry. Ruby, their fourteen-year-old daughter, or not their daughter, Ruby confided in me Cora is not her mother. She is likely another victim. Like Ella. She'll be in danger if they find out that I know the truth."

Even though I'd only met Ruby and sat with her a few times, I couldn't deny the connection the two of us had. I sensed there was something inside her — something dark, but not her soul, just like she had secrets. I had to save her.

Henry nodded. "She lives two doors down?"

"Yes. And I should confess... I broke in to their house looking for evidence that he'd taken Ella."

Henry looked surprised, his eyes widening even more. "What did you find?"

"Nothing. But when I was upstairs searching through the rooms, somebody threw rocks at the window right before the Gardenias came home. It was like a warning. Maybe it was Ruby. If so, she's in danger."

He chewed his bottom lip. "What day was this?"

"It's been two days. I can't let anything bad happen to Ruby." Dread filled my insides. What if they wanted to cover their tracks and to do that, they needed to get rid of Ruby?

"Call Detective White. Maybe he can help."

I nodded and hoped and maybe even prayed a little.

THIRTY-TWO

PACING AROUND MY LIVING ROOM, I was shaking my head in disbelief. "Detective White, it's him. I have an anonymous source, but I can give you the details. You just have to verify them officially. He flew from Seattle to Oakland International Airport on United Airlines two days before Ella went missing, and we have DMV records of him purchasing a white van. Just like the white van driven by the kidnappers. He was there. He had the opportunity. He had the means. The getaway car. His partner is his wife, Cora. She flew to the Bay Area with him. Neither had return tickets. They flew down there with the sole purpose of buying a van and kidnapping Ella. What more do you need?"

Trying to catch my breath, I couldn't believe Detective White wasn't jumping all over this. I admit it wasn't physical evidence, it was circumstantial. But it was far too coincidental to be an actual coincidence.

He said, "Allison, this is very compelling information. However, I'm concerned that you don't have official records."

"That's what I'm saying. I'll give you all the details so you can get warrants for the actual records. I'm the eye witness. That's probable cause, right? All you have to do is look."

I waited for his reply. He had to see that this was a huge break. "Okay, give me all the details, and I'll see what I can do. We'll pull the records, but I have to tell you — if it's a dead end and I can't corroborate your story, there's nothing more I can do."

A grin spread across my face. "That's fair. I promise, if this doesn't pan out, I won't bother you again."

"Okay. I'll get to it."

"Wait. There's more. I'm concerned Ella isn't the only girl he's taken. There's a young woman living in his house. Her name is Ruby, and she's fourteen years old. She looks exactly like Ella. Not exactly, exactly. Long strawberry blonde hair, blue eyes. I'm afraid they kidnapped her, too. Ruby has already confided in me that Cora is not her biological mother. I think Ruby is in danger."

"Let's start with you giving me the details about the travel, the van purchase, and their home address, and I'll have a patrol car check on Ruby."

"A patrol car? That will only make them nervous and suspicious."

"Okay. But I can't do a lot more than that right now. I have no evidence yet. As soon as I can corroborate your details, I promise I will fly to Seattle and question him myself."

Shaking my head back and forth, I couldn't believe he wasn't more excited about this. Or more concerned about Ruby. "All right, I'll let you know if I find anything else."

"As of this minute, I'm making this my top priority. I'll call as soon as I have more information."

I believed him but wasn't counting on him. "Thank you." I hung up and looked at Henry. "He's going to confirm the information officially. He says once he does that, he'll fly up to question Edison."

"That seems like a good start."

"If it's not too late." I glanced at my phone. Another text from Liam that said to call him. "I should call him back."

"Are you still dating him?"

"I don't know if I'm dating him. We've gone out, but we haven't since the police interrupted our last date. What if he knew his aunt had kidnapped my sister? I know it isn't likely, but how can I date someone who is related to my sister's kidnappers? But I should call back. I don't want to alarm him or his awful family."

"True."

Liam answered right away. "Are you okay?"

I shrugged, surprised that he was worried. "Why wouldn't I be okay?"

"You weren't at work yesterday, and you're working from home again today. Did something happen?"

"No, nothing happened."

"Are you sure? Because I think something happened with Ruby."

I turned and looked at Henry. "Why do you think something happened to Ruby?"

"I just got a message from my Aunt Cora, and she said to let you know Ruby can't meet with you anymore."

A heaviness filled my chest. Why would Cora want to keep Ruby away from me? "Did she say why?"

"No, but she seemed really upset. Did something happen?"

"No, of course not. I'm sorry, Liam. I have to go."

"Are you sure you're okay?"

"I'm sure. I'll call you later." I hung up, not waiting for a response. Did Cora know I was onto her? Did they know I suspected they had kidnapped Ruby? I explained the news to Henry.

"That sounds pretty suspicious."

"She's in trouble. I need to save her."

I may not have been able to save Ella, but I would save Ruby.

THIRTY-THREE

CORA

I FAKED my last smile for my last customer. Thankfully, the lunch rush at the bakery was busy enough that I could barely keep up with my own thoughts. Alone, I couldn't help but go back to the moment I saw the photo in Dorothy's hand and Ruby explaining where it came from. I'd fallen to my knees and passed out. When awakened, I begged Dorothy and Ruby not to tell Edison what they had found. I didn't want to think about what he would do to me if he knew Ruby knew his secret. Our secret.

I couldn't believe I didn't see it before. I should have known Allison was her sister. When she said Ruby looked so much like her, I should have known. Why had I been so stupid? So blind. More like blindsided. Never in all my dreams and nightmares did I think I would have to face her sister. Had Edison known it was her that day in the bakery? He must have. Or at least suspected. It would explain why he said he wouldn't be picking up Ruby anymore. He didn't want Allison to see him again.

Allison.

I used to tell myself I wasn't a bad person, but now I wasn't so sure. Here I was, keeping Ruby from Allison, hoping she wouldn't learn the truth. Did Allison already know? Surely if she did, she'd call the police or something. She wouldn't just keep eating my cupcakes and dating my nephew. Would she?

And then there was the reality that if anyone found out the truth, the cops would throw me in jail along with Edison. Maybe that was what we deserved. I certainly wasn't proud of what we had done. Not that Edison had given me a lot of choice in the matter. But I supposed I could have told him no. Or convinced him the plan would fail. I could've refused to go through with the plan. I could've refused at every single step, and I could've gone to the police. Would he have killed me if I had? Maybe. But was my life more important than the little girl's? I must have thought so. And I guess that made me a bad person. A coward. A frightened little bird, too scared of her overbearing husband to save a little girl. Yet, here I stood in my bakery. Alone. Completely capable of calling the police without fear of Edison coming after me. And I still did nothing.

Sometimes I wondered how I could've fallen so far from grace. I didn't even recognize myself anymore. Cupcake baker. Edison's doting wife. Ruby's adoring mother. None of it was real. Nothing in my life was real anymore.

Foolishly, I had thought the bakery was a beacon of hope. I couldn't change the past, but I could change things for Ruby.

It wasn't enough.

I knew I deserved everything that came to me, and probably more. But I wouldn't let it end at the hands of Edison. He had done too many horrible things to let him win. The door jingled, and I was thankful for another customer, another distraction. "Oh, hi, Liam."

"Hey. Looks like I missed the crowds."

"It's Friday. A lot of folks take the afternoon off to start their weekend early. Friday after lunch is the slowest time."

"Where's Ruby?"

"She doesn't work here anymore." I couldn't let Ruby get too close to Allison or anyone else. Having her there was a mistake. One that I may pay for the rest of my life. When I asked Ruby what Allison knew about our family, she had insisted she hadn't told Allison anything. But I couldn't take any chances.

"Oh, no. Why is that?"

"She decided she wanted to get ahead on her reading for public school." It was a terrible lie. It was one lie to cover the other lie — in perpetuity. I was surprised we'd been able to keep up with all the webs we had woven.

Liam's face scrunched up. "Is that why you won't let Ruby meet with Allison anymore? Because she's too busy with schoolwork?"

"Yes. I'm afraid she won't be as prepared as the other students who have been in the same public school since elementary school. She needs to catch up this summer."

Liam frowned, like he didn't believe me.

"Have you told Allison yet?" I hadn't seen her in the bakery. Liam hadn't mentioned her. Was it a coincidence that she had come in almost every day for cupcakes and lunch, but now she was MIA? That didn't make sense. What did she know?

"I told her. She seemed disappointed and wondered if she had done something wrong."

That poor Allison. I thought I couldn't hurt her any more than I had, but it turned out I could. "Oh no, it was nothing Allison did. Please assure her. I'm so grateful that she sat with Ruby and could mentor her. But now Ruby needs to focus on her current studies."

I thought I was a better liar, but it seemed like I needed to work on it. "Can I get you something? Late lunch? Cupcakes?"

"Just a turkey and avocado sandwich today."

"Coming right up." I walked behind to the sandwich preparation station and said, "I haven't seen Allison around and was worried she may have low blood sugar." I chuckled, trying to lighten the mood.

"She's been working from home."

"Oh, she's not sick, is she?"

"She is feeling a little under the weather."

"I'm so sorry to hear that. Maybe you can bring her a treat from us."

"Maybe I'll do that."

Liam was so sweet when he was little. I hadn't been a big part of his life since I was devoted to Edison. And he didn't like me visiting my sister, Liam's mother. What would Liam think of me if he knew the truth? I knew what he'd think of me. He would think I was a terrible excuse for a human being. One who didn't deserve to be among good people like him and Allison. He was right. I wasn't sure I could ever make up for what I had done. But maybe I could try.

I wrapped up the sandwich and placed it in the bag before reaching into the case and pulling out a pink lemonade cupcake and a red velvet. Allison liked both of them. I owed her more than a few cupcakes. I owed her twenty years of cupcakes.

When I'd agreed to the plan, I didn't think of all the people we would hurt. Obviously, I knew it would hurt the girl, but her family and her friends must have been forever altered. Hardened. I'd never had my own children — an inhospitable uterus, the doctor said. My desperation for a child was partially what led me to the worst mistake of my life.

I handed the bag to Liam and said, "Happy Friday."

"You too."

I smiled, trying to make it seem realistic, but as soon as he turned his head to walk out, my face fell, and the grief took over. If Liam found out, he would hate me, and it would likely ruin his relationship with Allison. It was like everything I touched turned rotten. Struggling not to cry, I failed.

Liam turned around as he reached for the door and stopped. He rushed back over. "Are you okay?"

"I'm fine." Wiping the tears from the corners of my eyes, I said, "It's just been a long week. I'm tired."

"Are you sure?"

I nodded. "Don't worry about me, Liam. I'll be okay." And I would. Because whatever was coming to me, I deserved it.

THIRTY-FOUR

SEATED at the dining table with Henry, I sipped my tea, knowing that anything caffeinated was more than I could handle. If anything, I needed a tranquilizer. Henry was a calming presence, but I thought he understood how close we were. "What do you want to do about Ruby?"

It was the question that had been bouncing around in my mind since I had ended the call with Detective White. "I don't know what I can do. I could go over to her house, but then what? Tell them I know Ruby's been kidnapped, and I'm taking her to the police? I offered that to her before, and she didn't want to go to the police."

Henry shook his head. "It would never work because she's never alone, right? She's at the bakery with Cora."

"That's exactly the problem. I need to get her away from them so I can make sure she's safe. But what if it's too late? I need to figure out a way to coax Ruby over here."

"Does she have a cell phone?"

"No. She told me she's not allowed and that even if she had one, she didn't have anyone to call."

"That's probably by design."

My phone buzzed, and I glanced down at the table. Another text message from Liam:

> Can I come over?

Absolutely not. Henry must've seen it too because he said, "Maybe you should call him, tell him not to come."

"You're right." I stood up and grabbed the phone. I had too much nervous energy to sit.

"Hi." He sounded out of breath.

"Hi, Liam. Now is not a good time for you to come over."

"What is going on, Allison? I just came from the bakery, and Cora had this weird story about Ruby staying home and studying for public high school. She's no longer working at the bakery."

I thought Liam said something else too, but all I could focus on was the fact that Ruby was not at the bakery. But Cora was and Edison was most likely at work, which meant Ruby was alone. This could be our one opportunity to save her. "Oh, that's really strange. Look, today's not a good day. I have a friend visiting from the Bay Area and..."

"A friend from the Bay Area?"

Shoot. On anybody else, it would have been a great excuse, but considering Liam and I had grown closer, it was out of the blue and suspicious. "Yeah, so that's one reason I'm working from home." I didn't want to let on that Henry was a man. It was too much to have to explain that we were just friends, and that would've been awkward and, frankly, none of his business.

"Okay. Well, Cora wanted me to drop off some cupcakes for you. I told her you weren't feeling well."

He lied for me? Was he suspicious of them, too? "You spoke to Cora about me?"

"Yeah, she said she hadn't seen you around and was worried."

Cora was worried about me? She noticed I had not been to the bakery. Did she know I suspected them? Did she finally figure out I was Ella's sister? What if they'd already hurt Ruby? "Well, thanks, but like I said, I have a guest over, and I really have to go. Thank you for thinking of me. We'll catch up another time."

"Oh, okay."

I hung up rather abruptly again. I probably needed to stop doing that, but I had bigger worries on my mind than whether I had upset Liam. "Ruby's home alone."

"Are you sure?"

"Not a hundred percent. But Liam said he was at the bakery and Ruby was not working there. Cora is and Edison should be at work. So, where else would she be?" That was an ominous question. What if she was no longer? What if, because of me, they killed her? I couldn't handle those types of thoughts. "We have to do something, Henry."

"We could go check on her. I can be the lookout and make sure the coast is clear. You can go in."

"You'd be willing to do that for me?"

"Sure."

Henry deserved a gold medal for the world's best friend. It was because of him I was finally going to learn the truth. I never had a friend like Henry before. I always had friends, but compared to Henry, they were more like surface level friends. Friends to go on trips with, or friends to share a good meal or a nice bottle of wine. Friends to go dancing with or friends to brunch with. They were good to have, but I'd never really opened up to any of them about the heartbreak I'd suffered when Ella was taken. None of them really understood how it affected me as much as Henry did. And maybe that's why he was my one true friend. All because of that one night we got drunk, and he told me his secrets, and I told him mine — that I was a phony who put on an act for the world to make it seem like I was normal and not broken inside. Maybe if I opened up to more people, I'd have more real friends. Or maybe my other friends would be scared off by how shattered I really was.

"Let's do it."

THIRTY-FIVE

ACTING CASUALLY, Henry and I strolled down the street as I pointed at trees and houses, as if giving him a tour of the neighborhood. As we approached the Gardenia home, I stopped and said, "Here it is."

"There are no cars in the driveway."

"They usually park in the garage."

"Okay, you stay here, and I'll check the garage."

"I broke the window when I was here last. I'm not sure if it's been fixed. It might be boarded up."

"I'll check it out." And with that, Henry hurried down the driveway as I surveyed for any potential witnesses. When I saw none, I continued up the walk to peer inside windows for any signs of the Gardenia adults or Ruby. The shades were drawn, but there didn't appear to be any lights on downstairs. Not that I could tell for sure, since it was daylight out, which meant maybe they didn't need them. Feeling unprepared for rescue missions and breaking and entering, I supposed a career in private investigation was out of the question. It was cool out, but I could already feel sweat dripping down my temples. I was not cut out for this.

The plan needed to work.

I glanced around the neighborhood, once more ensuring nobody was out and about. Luck was on my side, and I jogged over to the side of the house to meet Henry. He waved me over to the door with a sheet of plastic covering where glass had once been. "So, this is where you broke in?"

"Yep."

"I don't see any cars inside. With the plastic, it'll be easy to get in this way again."

"I don't want to scare Ruby. Let's check the back yard. Maybe we can see what is going on inside the house."

He pulled out his phone. "I'll stand watch. I'll text you if I see any cars approaching. Have your phone out."

I nodded and headed toward the backyard gate. I reached over and flipped the latch and slowly opened the wooden gate. Once through, I let it rest softly behind me, wiped my brow, and studied the back yard.

There were several structures that I hadn't noticed when I had run out in a panic. A shed with windows and a massive tent that looked like it could be used for storing firewood, but it was all enclosed in a strange fort-like structure. The property was much bigger than I had expected. Larger than my back yard. I continued to the side of the house and then the back, where I could see through the windows. There was no movement inside. And no sign of Ruby.

Back at the fence line, I glanced up toward the second floor to where Ruby's bedroom was situated. There was no sign of her there either, or anyone. *Please, don't let it be too late.*

Shaking my head, I tried to ignore all the thoughts associated with that. I had to focus on finding Ruby.

My phone buzzed and my pulse raced. Ugh. *Dr. Baker*

again. We had an appointment on Monday, so why was she calling me? If her little stunt with the police wasn't enough, now this. She was seriously getting on my last nerve. As far as I was concerned, she was the one with the mental problem. In the past five years, I'd reestablished my career, I owned my home, and I paid taxes. She needed to chill out.

Pressing the big red "ignore" button, I continue to look around when I thought I heard movement toward the far end of the back yard. My heart was now nearly pounding out of my chest. But I couldn't chicken out now. What if the sound was Edison doing something terrible to Ruby? Maybe I should get Henry. No, he was the lookout. He would tell me if somebody was coming. There were no cars, so it couldn't be Edison out there. I crept closer, and the door to the shed opened up. It was Ruby.

A wide smile appeared on her face. "Allison." She jogged toward me and wrapped her arms around me. I hugged her back.

With a mix of shock and relief, I stepped back. "You're okay?"

"Yes, what are you doing here? I mean, I'm glad you are, but—"

There was a look in her eyes that I couldn't quite figure out. Excitement? Joy?

"Liam told me you weren't at the bakery and that I wasn't allowed to meet with you anymore. I was worried about you. You know you can tell me anything. I will do everything I can to protect you."

She nodded, and a small tear escaped her eye. "I know you will. I wasn't sure if I could trust you before. I wasn't sure it was you, but now I know. She confirmed it, but I didn't have a way to contact you. We thought of going to your house, but she was too scared. She hasn't left in so long."

I shook my head. "I don't understand what you're saying."

She looked at the watch on her wrist. "We don't have a lot of time."

"Time for what?"

"We have to get out of here. You said you would help us?"

"Us?"

She nodded and grabbed my hand. She led me over to the shed and opened the door. "It's okay to come out."

A woman's voice said, "Are you sure?"

I gasped and covered my mouth with my hand.

Ruby turned back to me. "Are you alone?"

In a state of shock, I was about to say yes, but then I remembered Henry. I lowered my hand. "My friend Henry is out front. He's the lookout. I was kinda planning to break in again."

"Again?" Ruby chuckled. "I heard about that. We can talk about it later. Can we trust Henry?"

"I would trust Henry with my life. He knows everything. He said he would text if anybody comes near the house."

"Good. That's perfect." She grabbed my hand and stared up at the sky. "Thank you, God."

Oh, no. Had I stumbled into some weird religious cult? That didn't matter. If they were trying to escape, I would help. As I pondered everything that I'd heard and seen in the last minute, a woman stepped out of the shed.

Our eyes met.

My mouth dropped open, and my chest constricted. I tried to speak, and I couldn't. I didn't know if the vision in front of me was real.

Ruby said, "When you gave me the picture of your sister and you, I showed it to her. I had to be sure."

My eyes returned to the woman's bright blue ones, her peaches and cream complexion with freckles across the bridge of her nose and long strawberry blonde hair that went down to her waist. There were little creases near the edges of her eyes that weren't there before. She was twenty years older, but I would know my sister anywhere. "Ella?"

Tears streamed down my face as Ella nodded. "How did you find me?" Ella broke into tears as she wrapped her arms around me. I stood there for I don't know how long as the rest of the world disappeared, and it was just me and my sister, hugging, crying.

She stepped back.

"It's really you?" I cried.

She nodded. "It's me."

"How long have you been here?" Was that a stupid question? It didn't matter.

"Almost twenty years."

It had never crossed my mind that she could be two doors down — still with Edison. Why didn't she escape? She reached for Ruby and put her arm around her shoulder and squeezed her close and kissed her on the forehead. As if reading my mind, Ella said, "Before Ruby was born, I wanted to escape. I tried a few times, but then Ruby came along, and I could never leave her."

Never leave her? I looked at Ella and Ruby and back again. Ella nodded. "Ruby is my daughter."

Speechless. I had a thousand questions. But now wasn't the time. All I knew was that Ella was alive and her sneaky, brilliant daughter brought us together. "I'm an auntie?"

Ruby nodded. "I think you're the best auntie ever."

Overwhelmed, I stared at her. She had been excited. That was the look in her eyes. She knew we were going to be reunited. Ruby said, "We don't have a lot of time. Cora will be home any minute."

Looking back at Ella, I never wanted to see anything else. "I never gave up, Ella. I never accepted you were gone. Never."

"How did you end up here? Two doors down?"

"I don't know. I thought the house was cool. There was something about the house. I had never even been here. My realtor showed me a video, and that was it. Something about the house told me it was the right one."

Ella said, "God brought you here."

I hadn't believed in such a thing since the day Ella went missing, but I supposed, like my faith that Ella wasn't gone, maybe God was real, too.

My phone buzzed. A message from Henry.

A gray SUV is coming down the road.

"A gray SUV."

"That's Cora's," Ruby said. "We have to get out of here."

THIRTY-SIX

CORA

BEWILDERED, I watched the Asian man with short dark hair, wearing a hoodie, standing at the end of my driveway, waving at someone. Who was he? Was he the burglar back to finish the job? Who was he waving to? There was more than one criminal. Grabbing for my phone to call the police, I stopped when the three figures jogging toward him emerged from the back yard. The man's dark eyes met mine, and he yelled something that looked like he was telling them to run faster. I stopped my car right in the street, turned off the engine, and ran over to the group fleeing from my home. I rushed over to Ruby, Dorothy, and Allison.

"What are you doing?" I glanced at Allison, who had a look of fury in her eyes. *Oh, no.* What did she know? I knew I should not have let Ruby stay home. I had been worried Allison would influence her or find out our secrets. They didn't have a way of communicating. So, why was Allison at our house? And more concerning, why was she holding Dorothy's hand?

Allison said, "Get out of our way."

"You can't just leave, that's my daughter."

She spat, "No, she's not. She's my niece. Ella's daughter. I know everything. Get out of the way, or you will be sorry."

It was one of those moments in life that defines you. I knew what they were like and how it could change you. I'd had one before — twenty years earlier. And this would be another one that could define the next twenty. Would I fight or let justice be served, even if that meant my demise? "Can't we just talk about this?"

If they went to the police, I would likely spend the rest of my life behind bars. Knowing I was in better hands with the police than Edison, I tried to reason with them, but I didn't know how. How had Allison found out about Ruby? How did Ruby know? We had been so careful. She wasn't ever supposed to know Dorothy was her mother.

Ruby shook her head. "Look, Cora, Allison knows everything. She knows that Dorothy, actually Ella, is her sister and that you and Dad kidnapped her and that I am her daughter, not yours. There's nothing you can do to stop us."

My energy drained. How could I fight that? How could I possibly argue with that logic? I had no claim to Ruby despite what I had told everybody the last fourteen years. Ruby was the reason I had gone along with Edison's plan. He told me we could find a young woman and she could have a baby that I could raise as my own. When he told me about a young woman, he hadn't explained it was actually a fourteen-year-old girl. I didn't realize his true proclivities until after we had driven away with Dorothy restrained in the back seat. I'll never forget the moment I realized what we had done.

A few hours after driving up north, we had stopped, and when I got a really good look at the girl, my heart had sunk. She was so young. A baby. A terrified little girl. On the side of the road, outside the van, I'd argued with Edison that she was too young and that we had to take her back. He explained a young one was the plan all along and that I was nuts for thinking he would want an older woman. He already had one of those and she was defective. He said it was luck we had happened upon the girl. We had only planned to pick up some groceries when he spotted her. He tried to convince me it was a sign she was the right one. Broken, I knew we had already passed the point of no return.

In that moment, the house of cards I was living in collapsed. I did not know that day would reveal who my husband really was. Sure, I knew he was controlling and didn't have a pure heart, but I did not know he was a pedophile. After we had gotten home with Ella, we forced her to choose a new name. She chose Dorothy. And then he took her into one of the back rooms by himself. All I could hear was crying and the tell-tale signs of Edison's gratification.

When I realized what was happening, I climbed into the shower, sobbing and shaking, until I had nothing left inside of me. I was so ashamed of what I had done. How could I have been so stupid and so selfish to think it was okay to abduct a young woman so that I could be a mother? I wondered if that's why God hadn't blessed me with a child in the first place, because God knew I was the type of person who would allow her husband to abduct a young girl and rape her over and over while keeping her chained in a tent in the back yard.

The early years were the most horrifying, and I admit I turned to the bottle, trying to forget what we had done.

After she aged out of his fantasies, he impregnated her. The poor girl didn't even know what was happening until she was about five months along. Once we saw the positive pregnancy test, Edison left her alone. I always wanted to ask her if she was relieved, but I knew I didn't deserve answers. Dorothy deserved better. Over the years, guilt overtook me, and I had convinced Edison to build a more comfortable home for her. A solid structure with air conditioning and heating and a small bathroom. It was the least I could do.

When Ruby was about a year old, Edison decided she would live in the house with us, and Dorothy would act as if she were a babysitter or nanny. We instructed Ruby to call me Mom and Dorothy stopped breastfeeding her. Ruby was to never know the truth. Looking at Ruby and Dorothy now, I realized there was no way Ruby believed I was her mother. She probably never had.

Over the years, Dorothy, Ruby, Edison, and I acted like an unconventional family of sorts. He instructed us to refer to Dorothy as the neighbor, since she lived in her own dwelling. She didn't seem to hate us, which I always found strange because I think that if I was in Dorothy's situation, I would hate me. Frankly, I hated myself.

Dorothy stared directly into my eyes. "Cora, there's nothing left to discuss. We're leaving, and we're not coming back."

Gripped with fear, I shifted my gaze to Ruby and said, "What about your dad?"

Ruby shook her head. "My dad is a monster, and you know it. I've always known Dorothy is my real mother. I want nothing to do with a man who would kidnap a young girl, a girl my age, Cora! And keep her captive. For all I care, he can go to hell."

I stepped back, shocked by Ruby's words. She had always been so sweet and so kind. Had it all been an act? Had she been waiting for this moment her whole life? I had always thought she was a daddy's girl. Maybe she was just playing the part, not wanting to rock the boat. I pleaded, "Let me help."

Allison stepped forward, protecting her sister and niece with her body. "I think you've done enough, Cora."

The next moments were a blur. All I could remember was crying, "I'm sorry," over and over as they left me standing there. Alone. After my tears dried, the fear took over, and I wondered what would happen next. What would Edison do when he found out? Would he get to me before the police did?

THIRTY-SEVEN

AFTER SEEING CORA, a red-hot rage had replaced the elation that I had found my sister. My anger toward Cora, a woman who had not only kidnapped my teenage sister and stood by as her husband did horrible things to her but also stole Ella's child and pretended Ruby was her own, was barely comprehensible. What kind of person would do that? In my book, she was almost worse than Edison. Almost.

All I had was speculation about what had turned Cora into the monster she had become. Was she a victim of domestic violence? Maybe she was, or maybe she wasn't. I didn't know, but I had a difficult time having any sympathy for somebody who could do what they did to my sister, my flesh and blood. Or to anyone, for that matter.

Not knowing what time Edison would be home, I buried the fury and used all of my energy to dash toward my house to save my sister and niece. *Niece. I have a niece.*

All four of us reached the house without incident and were cozy in my living room with the security system armed. My heart was beating so fast I worried I would pass out.

There were so many emotions filling my insides, I couldn't help but stand and stare at Ella and Ruby. It was like a dream, like I was living somebody else's life. Like the *before* times.

Henry put his hand on my shoulder. "Should we call the police?"

I turned to Henry. "Yes, we should." Turning to Ella and Ruby, I said, "Is it okay with you if we call the police? I've been in contact with the original detective on Ella's case and have told him about Edison. His name is Detective White, and he's never given up on finding you either."

Huddled with Ruby, Ella nodded. "You can call."

The love I felt for Ella and Ruby filled me up, pushing out the years of anger and heartbreak.

Henry said, "Do you want me to call?"

"If you don't mind." Glancing at my family, I realized I had never introduced Henry. "And sorry, Henry, this is Ella, my sister, and my niece, Ruby. This is Henry. He's my best friend in the entire world, and he helped me find you."

Ruby smirked. "I figured. But, hi, Henry. It's nice to meet you and thank you."

Such a teenager. *I love it.*

Ella said, "It's nice to meet you. Thank you. Thank you both." She teared up again.

"It's my pleasure."

About to hand him my phone, I wrapped my arms around him. "Thank you so much. How will I ever repay you?"

He must have sensed I was about to break down because he patted me on the shoulder, stepped back, and said, "There is plenty of time for that. Plus, you bought me Reese's and gave me unlimited coffee. I'd say we're even."

All of us laughed at his silliness. I didn't think we'd ever be even. Before handing him my phone, I scrolled through my contacts, clicked on Detective White, and let it call. Ruby, Ella, and I sat on the couch and waited.

Henry said, "Hi. Is this Detective White? Yes, I'm a friend of Allison Smythe. I'm with her right now. She asked me to call to tell you we found her. We found Ella." And then he went off to describe all the details from the moment he arrived in Seattle until now.

Henry nodded and nodded before finally looking over at me. "Do you want to talk to the detective?"

"Okay."

He handed me the phone.

"Your friend just told me quite the story."

"It's unbelievable, Detective White, but she's okay. You're okay, right, Ella?"

In a whisper, Ella said, "I'm more than okay."

Detective White asked, "That was Ella?"

"Yes, she's here, and her daughter Ruby, too. She has a daughter. She's fourteen. Do you remember me telling you about Ruby? They didn't kidnap her; she's my sister's daughter. My niece." I didn't think I would ever tire of those words. *My niece.*

"I do. May I speak with Ella?"

"Hold on." I lowered the phone. "Ella, are you okay talking to the detective?"

She nodded.

"She says it's okay, but what should we do? I have the alarm set. Should I call the local police?"

"Let me talk to Ella. After I talk to her, I'll call the local police. We'll take care of everything."

"Okay."

I passed the phone to Ella, and she said, "Hello."

Ella was brave as she provided the details of her kidnapping, of where she was being held captive, and the names of those who took her. Part of me didn't think I was as strong as she was. Listening to the details of what had happened in the last twenty years made me physically ill. My poor Ella. I would let nothing bad happen to her ever again. Or I'd at least try my best to protect her and Ruby.

We sat silently until Ella finished her conversation with Detective White. She returned the phone to me.

"I can't believe you found her. I'm so glad." His voice cracked before he paused and said, "It's a miracle."

Detective White had told me during a few conversations that Ella's case was one he could never let go and that he would never give up trying to find her.

"Do you feel calm enough to drive to the police station?"

After a sniffle and a deep breath, I said, "Probably, but maybe Henry wouldn't mind driving us."

Henry said, "I can drive."

"My friend Henry said he will drive."

"Good. He sounds like a good friend. I want for all of you to go to the Seattle Police Department. By the time you get there, I'll have called ahead and will confirm there will be an officer and support staff waiting for you. In the event that Edison comes home, I think it's best to leave right away."

"Okay."

"We'll be in touch."

"Wait."

"What is it?"

"I have to call my mom." The tears were reemerging as I looked over at Ella and Ruby.

"Can you call her on the drive there? Or wait until you get to the police station."

"It will take about ten minutes to get there."

"I'll ask the officers in charge to give you a private room. You can call your mom as soon as you get to the police station."

I nodded and then verbally said yes and ended the call. "We need to go to the Seattle Police Department right away to make sure that we all stay safe."

Ruby and Ella stood up. They were ready. If I had to guess, I would think they had been waiting for this day for a long time. Henry said, "We can take my car."

Nobody needed any further instruction. We hurried to Henry's car. I turned toward the Gardenia house and saw that Cora had pulled her car into the driveway. I didn't see any sign of Edison, but there were dark clouds looming overhead.

Inside, I sat in the front seat as Ella and Ruby sat in the back seat holding hands. The entire time, I was turned in my seat, fixated on them. "I'm so happy I found you. Ruby, my gosh, my niece. I knew there was something about you when I first met you."

"That's when I first suspected that maybe you knew Dorothy."

"Dorothy?"

She shook her head. "Sorry, habit."

Ella said, "They made me change my name shortly after they took me. They told me I could pick any name I wanted, so I picked Dorothy from the Wizard of Oz. There's no place like home, right?"

I thought my heart couldn't break any more. The thought of my teenage sister, wishing she were in a movie and could click her heels three times and be home, tore me up. "We'll go home soon. Mom never sold the house after..." Ella didn't know our father had died.

"After what?"

"Dad died earlier this year. But Mom is still there, and we can call her at the station."

Ella stared at me and said, "I dreamed of this day. I can't believe it's here," as she clung to Ruby.

The two were never to be separated.

I was sure Ella had so many stories about her captivity, but now wasn't the time. I just wanted to be with my sister and to call my mom. "The police are probably going to ask you a lot of questions. Is that okay?"

"I've been waiting a long time to tell my story."

She was obviously more prepared for all of this than I was. Parked in the lot at the police station, Henry said, "We're here."

Henry, my hero. What would I have done without him?

We exited the car and walked hand-in-hand, Ella, me, and Ruby. Henry led the way like a gallant soldier protecting us. If you didn't know him, Henry wasn't much to look at. You wouldn't think he was a defender and protector of the innocent. He was slight of build and 5'7", but he had the spirit of a warrior. Henry held open the door for us as we entered the station.

In front of us stood three people who apparently had been waiting for us. Two middle-aged men in wrinkled dark suits, and a young-ish woman wearing a gray suit. The first two introduced themselves as detectives and last, the woman said she was with victim services.

We introduced ourselves, and they greeted us warmly with handshakes and smiles, but when they reached Ella and Ruby, there wasn't a dry eye in sight. Detective White was right. It was a miracle, and these detectives knew it too. I glanced around the police station and saw others had stood up to watch us. They wore smiles and nodded their joy toward us. Suddenly, the enormity of the situation became very clear. Ella wasn't just our miracle; she was a symbol of hope.

Detective Berry said, "We spoke with Detective White, and he said that you would like to call your mother before we question Ella. We have a room waiting for you. Can I get any of you anything — water, soda, snacks, dinner, or a blanket? You name it, it's yours."

We thanked them, and after we requested water and dinner, Detective Berry took us into a room that had a small sofa, table, and chairs. "We'll be right outside the door, protecting you. Nobody will get past me. Take all the time you need."

"Thank you."

Henry said, "I'll give your family some space. I'll go help get food."

"You can stay if you like. If you ask me, I'd say you're part of the family now."

"Thank you."

The officer nodded and closed the door.

With shaking hands, I pulled out my phone and Facetimed my mom. Mom's beaming face appeared. "Allison, what a surprise. How are you, honey? Are you crying? What's wrong? Is everything okay?"

My emotions were preventing me from speaking for a good while. I finally choked out, "We found her."

"What are you saying? What do you mean?" The tears were already in her eyes.

"Ella. I found Ella. She's here with me."

Mom was shaking her head in disbelief. I don't know if I would have believed it either. "I don't understand."

Ella scrunched next to me, and I backed off so Mom could get a good look at her. "Hi, Mom."

Mom and Ella both broke down, unable to speak. After a minute, Ruby called out, "I'm here, too."

My mom stopped crying and said, "Who's that?"

Ella moved the phone over so that Ruby was in the frame with her. "This is my daughter, Ruby."

At first, I wasn't sure if the screen had frozen or the call had ended, but soon I realized Mom was just frozen with shock. "My granddaughter. Hi, Ruby."

"Hi," Ruby said with a wide smile.

There were voices in the background. Mom wasn't alone. Soon, she was explaining the situation to someone. When I caught her attention, I quickly filled her in on the events of the day and our current location. Without hesitation she said, "I'll book a flight. Regina is coming with me. Right, Regina?"

I heard a faint, "Of course," from Regina, one of my mom's best friends and a neighbor.

Henry said, "I can meet her at the airport."

"Who was that? Was that Liam?"

Liam. "That's my friend Henry from college. He's been helping me find Ella."

"Well then, thank you, Henry!" she shouted.

Henry smiled at the camera phone, pointed at him.

After a few more moments of staring at each other, Mom said, "Honey, I'm going to call the airline so I can be there right away, and then I'll call right back."

Ella said, "Talk to you soon, Mom."

And just like that, my family was back together.

THIRTY-EIGHT

CORA

With dry eyes and an empty heart, I studied the home that I had built with Edison. A house filled with deception and abuse. Nothing could make up for what I had done, and nothing could make it right, but I knew how to make things worse. Ella and Ruby would not suffer another moment because of me. It was time to face the music and admit what I had done. The plan was to tell the authorities everything I knew about what had happened in the last thirty-five years that I had spent with Edison.

Ella was the only girl he had taken and brought back home, but I suspected there were other victims. I didn't know their names or fates, but over the years, I had kept records of Edison's trips with special notes when he'd come home in a better mood than when he'd left. Hopefully, those details would help the police with unsolved crimes. Edison was too evil to have hurt just one girl. And it was time for him to pay for what he had done.

My purse clutched in my arms, I figured I didn't need to

bring anything with me other than my identification, phone, and notes on Edison from over the years. I took a deep breath and looked at my house for what I suspected would be the very last time.

A silent goodbye.

This wasn't the first time I had considered turning us in to the police. Over the years, I wondered if I had the courage to do it. Obviously, I hadn't. But it was different now. We were already found out. It was time. I had pictured it all in my mind of how it would go down. I'd walk through the door of the police station and talk to someone behind the desk and say I needed to talk to a detective and then, seated across from a man with a mustache in a cheap suit, I would tell him everything.

No details left out.

I had to make sure Edison was put away forever and couldn't hurt anyone ever again. But I wasn't stupid and knew that in doing that, I sealed my fate, but I sealed my fate long ago. I grabbed the sweater draped over the back of the couch and slung it over my arm. I was finally ready to do the right thing.

At the sound of footsteps at the door, my heart thumped. Had they come for me already?

But then I heard the key insert and turn. *No.* The door opened, and Edison looked me up and down. "Going somewhere?"

"I'm just going to the grocery store. I need to pick up a few things for dinner. I'll be back in just a little while." Stuttering, I had tried to sound confident but failed.

"Ruby isn't going with you?"

She normally would have. It was one of the few outings she could partake in. "No, she has some things to do."

Edison barely shrugged as he walked into the living room

and called out for Ruby. Not to my surprise, but to Edison's, there was no call back.

Heart pounding, I watched Edison's every move until he locked eyes with mine. And as if he knew all about my plan, he ran up the stairs, yelling Ruby's name, and then ran back down the stairs. He rushed toward the back yard, flung open the slider, and ran toward Dorothy's house, still yelling Ruby's name. I hurried over to see what he did next. He kicked in Dorothy's door and began screaming Dorothy's name.

I should have run. I should have acted. That had always been my weakness. Not acting when I knew I should.

I knew he'd be back for me, and he was. He sprinted back into the house, face crimson, with the devil in his eyes. He yelled, "Where are they? What have you done?"

Backing away, I said, "It's over, Edison. It's over."

"Where are they?"

"They're gone. It's over." He obviously wasn't understanding what I was trying to say.

"Cora, I will ask you one more time. Where are Ruby and Dorothy?"

"They left with Allison and some Asian man. They know Allison is Dorothy's sister. Ruby knows everything. It's over."

His eyes grew wide, and his hands clenched into fists. "This is all your fault." He grabbed me by my hair and slammed me to the ground. "You stupid woman. How could you let this happen? This is all your fault," he repeated while he kicked me in the ribs.

The pain felt like knives stabbing my insides. I lost count of how many times he kicked me, but after one last kick to my back, he rushed up the stairs. My phone had fallen out of my purse, but it was within reach. I winced in pain as I reached for the phone. Liam had texted. I pressed his name and then the call button.

He answered, and I cried, "Help."

But before I could explain, Edison swiftly grabbed the phone out of my hand and stomped it. And the next thing I saw was his boot before everything went dark.

THIRTY-NINE

WE ATE a hearty dinner of fettuccini Alfredo, pizza, and green salad. I ate three times my normal amount of food. All the activity and emotions from the day had distracted me from eating anything since breakfast. As we ate, there was no concern about calories or working it off at the gym the next day. Ella hadn't eaten pizza since her abduction and was excited to have pepperoni and olive, her favorite. I marveled as she picked off the olives with her fork before taking a bite into the now pepperoni only pizza. It was exactly how she had eaten it when we were kids. I used to tease her but smiled, as Ruby had taken over the role.

After our initial tearful hellos, hugs, and lingering stares, we spent our time stuffing our faces and talking about the things we liked and what we had in common. Normal stuff.

We didn't discuss the trauma that the two girls had gone through. It wasn't the time, and I didn't know what the protocol was. Surely they would both need therapy. I *wouldn't* be recommending Dr. Baker. But he had hidden them away from the world for so long that it had to impact them. Although my impression of Ruby was that she would be just fine. She was an outgoing teenager who appeared to be resilient, thoughtful, and intelligent.

Ella, I worried about. She was quieter than she used to be, understandably, but still upbeat and looking forward to a life on the outside, as she called it. But I could feel the pain I saw in her eyes that wasn't there when she was younger. It was as if a little of her sparkle had dimmed. I hoped it would return.

The officers told us to take all the time we needed but had confided in me when they brought dinner that nobody on staff was going home until they interviewed Ella and Ruby. Part of me didn't want to let it happen. I didn't want either of them out of my sight. It was too raw. We were too close to being together for the rest of our lives. I couldn't imagine us being apart again. But I knew this was our new beginning, not the end.

My phone buzzed. I looked to see if it was Mom calling to say that she had arrived at the Oakland airport to head up to Seattle, but it was Liam. I ignored it. What would I say to him? "Stop calling me. I really liked you, but your aunt and uncle stole my sister and held her captive for twenty years." I supposed eventually that was exactly what I needed to explain. One day.

A few moments later, another buzz. A text from Liam:

Call me back. It's an emergency.

An emergency? Pushing myself off the chair, I called him. "What is it?"

"Where are you?"

"I'm not at home." This wasn't the time for a full-blown explanation.

"I just got a really distressing call from Cora. She said that she needed help. But then the phone went dead. Are you at home so you can go check on her? She may be in danger."

Maybe she would get what she deserved. I couldn't contemplate that at the moment. "It's Edison. He's dangerous."

Ella gave me a knowing look.

"What do you mean? You're wrong about him."

Through gritted teeth, I said, "No, I'm not. He's terrible. We are currently at the police station. I will let an officer know Cora needs help." I hung up the phone.

Liam was sweet but maybe a little too naïve. Edison was a monster. I shouldn't be angry at Liam, but he barely knew Edison, so why was he being so defensive? Was it simply because he thought I was crazy?

I looked at my group. "That was Liam. Cora called him. All she said was that she needed help before the line went dead. I need to let the police know she could be in danger. I'll be right back."

Both Ella and Ruby looked worried. Did they care for Cora, even after what she'd done? I couldn't think about that. I hurried out of the room and went up to the front desk.

"Ms. Smythe, is everything okay?"

"No, Cora Gardenia's nephew just called me..." I explained everything to the officer.

Detective Berry popped up from behind me. "We'll send a team over there. Gardenia may try to cover his tracks."

That was what I was worried about. I didn't want him to get away.

Detective Berry gave orders to the officer behind the desk and then turned back to me. "How are things going in there?"

I understood the subtext. They had been waiting for us for over an hour. "We've just finished dinner. Everyone's good. I think they're ready to talk to you."

"Great. And how are you holding up? It's been quite the day."

That made me want to break down and cry. "I'm okay. It's been a good day. But a long day, too."

"I'm sure. When will your mom get here?"

"Her flight leaves in about an hour. So, hopefully before midnight."

"Good. We might be able to send you home by then."

Panic set in. We were safe in the police station, but what about two doors down from the monster?

"We'll have officers outside your house if we don't have them in custody by then."

"Thanks."

"We'll be by in a few minutes to talk to Ella and Ruby."

I said, "I'll let them know," and hurried back to my sister, my niece, and Henry. Ella and Ruby watched me as I walked back into the room and shut the door behind me. "They're sending help to the Gardenia house."

Ruby said, "He got to her. He must've found out we were gone, and he got her."

"Was he violent?" I was afraid to ask but knew I had to.

Ruby answered, "Never with me, but Cora and I always had to do exactly what he said. And there were times I saw him hit Cora. It would be a small thing, like he said he didn't want extra oregano in the spaghetti sauce, but he thought she had added extra and smacked her right at the dining table. He was violent, and he was controlling. I didn't want to be his daughter." And with that, Ruby cried. Not happy tears. Maybe Cora was a victim, just like Ella and Ruby.

Maybe I shouldn't hate Cora. She let them go, and she said sorry. Like she had regrets, but she was still culpable, right? "Was Cora nice to you?"

Ella stroked Ruby's hair, and she calmed. Ella explained,

"She wasn't like Edison, but she didn't stop it, either. At first, she didn't like that I was there. I couldn't blame her for that. Her husband had other *interests* in her own house." Ella blushed. "But she was never mean unless she was following orders from Edison. He was not nice. He took what he wanted and did what he wanted, and it didn't matter what anybody else wanted. He was nice to Ruby, though."

For the first time that day, I saw a flicker of anger in Ella's eyes.

Ruby shrugged. "He was never mean, but he was very strict. He wouldn't let me leave the house or go to regular school, but over the last few years, he kind of loosened the reins a bit and let Cora open the bakery. Cora had never been so happy. My whole life, I thought she was a really unhappy person, but when she opened the bakery, it changed her."

But she still kept my sister and niece in captivity. If what they said was true, Cora was a victim, but something told me she wasn't completely innocent. Hopefully, the police arrived in time and she was safe. But how safe could anybody be in the hands of a monster like Edison?

The door opened, and it was Detective Berry and his partner. "If you're ready, Ella, you can come with me. And Ruby, you can go with my partner."

Both women nodded and Ella asked, "Did you find Cora?"

"Last I heard, they're on the scene. I don't know her status yet."

Ella looked stricken as she and Ruby followed the detectives out of the room.

Alone with Henry, I said, "Have I thanked you enough for being here?"

"You don't have to keep thanking me."

"Seriously? I feel like I owe you a house or something."

Henry chuckled. "Unnecessary. I already have one. But I

can stay as long as you need me. And I can pick up your mom. I can tell you don't want to leave your sister."

"Am I that obvious?"

"It's understandable. How are you feeling? You must be so overwhelmed."

Overwhelmed was an understatement. "I'm happy. Tired. I'll be okay."

"What about Liam? What are you going to do about him?"

"I liked him, but there's no future there. I couldn't possibly date him now." As if on cue, the door opened and an officer in uniform said, "Ms. Smythe, there is someone named Liam Parker here to see you."

Right. I had told him I was at the police station. "Can you have him come back here?"

"Sure."

Shaking my head, I realized this was happening today. A few moments later, Liam entered, stricken by the fact we were sitting in the police station, and I was with a strange man, Henry. "Hi. I just wanted to see if you're okay?"

"I'm fine." I went on to explain everything that had happened that day and everything we knew about Ella's abduction. He sat down on the couch, pale. He hadn't known. Sitting with his head in his hands, he looked tormented. I felt bad for him, but I had other things I had to focus on.

He lifted his head. "I'm sorry I didn't believe you. I'm sure you never want to see me again, which sucks because I really care for you, Allison."

He was right, and it sucked. "They sent help to Cora's house. I haven't heard any updates, though."

He shrugged. "It's strange. They seemed happy. They seemed normal. Never in a million years would I have thought they were capable of this." He shook his head again in disbelief. "Is there anything I can get you? Anything I can do to help?"

"No, I have Henry." Before he could contemplate whether Henry was my secret boyfriend, I said, "He's a friend from college. He was helping me look into the background of your uncle. He found some things that prove he took Ella."

"We're just friends," Henry assured him.

"Henry is more like family."

Despite the explanation, Liam looked hurt and disappointed. I couldn't really worry about that right now. I had my sister and niece, and my mom was arriving soon. He slapped his hands on his thighs and stood up. "Okay, call me if you need anything."

I stood up. "Thank you, Liam."

He lowered his head. "Take care, Allison."

Watching him leave, I wondered if it would be the last time I would ever see him.

FORTY

After hours at the police station, exhaustion took over. My body longed for sleep and the comfort of my bed, but at the same time, I was conflicted because I didn't want to leave Ella and Ruby. Although the two had survived the past twenty years without me. *They're tough.* Would my bed fit all three of us? Probably not. I had a guest room Henry was staying in. Where would Mom, Ella, and Ruby sleep? I could take the couch. After everything we had gone through that day, it likely wasn't that big of a deal, and I didn't need to worry. We'd figure it out.

Before we left the station, the victims' advocate hooked us up with some names and numbers of therapists and reunification specialists for us to contact. Ella and Ruby also met with a few specialists before we left the station to make sure they were mentally and physically healthy. They were deemed acceptable and told me they desperately wanted to go home. I wasn't sure what they meant, but they quickly explained they meant my home. My house was new to me and them, but we were together, and that's what made it home.

Driving through our neighborhood, with Henry behind the

wheel, I wondered what had happened with Edison and Cora. Detective Berry said they would contact me when there was an update. It had been hours. Why weren't they in jail? Had they fled?

Wonder turned to shock as we reached my house, and we could see at least two dozen police cars blocking the road surrounding the Gardenias'. Ella and Ruby had squished over to one side of the car to peer outside the window to see. I said, "Henry, park in the driveway, and then we can go see what's going on."

"Are you sure that's a good idea?"

Was it a good idea? Maybe, maybe not. But how could we just waltz into my house without knowing more? We'd made it this long, we had to find out what was happening. Plus, I could tell by the words they had said earlier, and the looks in their eyes, both Ella and Ruby were concerned about Cora.

Parked, the four of us hopped out of the car and jogged toward the police barricade. As we approached, a uniformed officer put his hands out, telling us to stop. "You can't be here. I need you to go back to your house and lock the doors."

"Is Detective Berry here?" I asked.

He gave me a quizzical look. Ella stepped forward. "I live there."

Ruby did the same. "Me too."

The cop looked confused as he furrowed his brow. He was obviously flummoxed by what was going on. He pulled out his radio and asked for Detective Berry. Moments later, Detective Berry ran toward us. "You shouldn't be here."

"What's going on, detective?" Ella asked.

"I'll tell you the current situation, but then I need you to go to Allison's house and get comfortable. Get some rest. Plus, you need to wait for your mom. She's flying in tonight, right?"

He was right. "Her flight gets in soon."

"Henry, you plan to pick her up?"

Henry said, "We decided we would all go, but I'll be driving, sir."

"Good. All right, I need you to stay here, but I'll tell you what we've got going on right now. We believe Cora Gardenia is inside the home and that she is gravely injured or deceased. Edison is inside. He has a weapon, and he hasn't come out yet. We have a hostage negotiator on the scene trying to work with him to come out peacefully. Now, I need you to go to Allison's and lock the doors until you leave for the airport."

My knees weakened. After everything we'd endured that day, it was crazy to think it could end this way. Had Cora lost her life? Was I sad? I supposed in a way I was sad for anybody who passed before their time. But there was nothing extra for Cora. Before we could argue, someone yelled, "He's coming out!" And then, "He's got a gun!"

Detective Berry yelled at us, "Get down!"

As we kissed the pavement, pops rang out like firecrackers that detonated too close to our ears. The air filled with smoke as the battle seemed to go on for an eternity, but in reality, it was less than a minute. Fear gripped my insides, but I crept up to check on Ella and Ruby. Detective Berry commanded, "Stay down," before he frog crawled toward the Gardenia house.

We waited with cheeks on the pavement until an officer approached us. "It's all clear. You can get up. Detective Berry will be over shortly."

The four of us exchanged silent glances. We were all okay. Nobody was hit. I looked back at the scene and waited for Detective Berry.

All clear could only mean one thing. Edison was no longer a threat, and neither was Cora. Were they dead?

We group-hugged, and I felt like we had avoided death. That might be dramatic, but this whole day had felt like we had been running a marathon that was literally life or death. I found my sister after twenty years and my niece that I didn't know I had but loved instantly. I had a friend who I realized was more like a brother, someone I could always count on for anything.

We released one another and braced ourselves for news of what had happened. Detective Berry jogged toward us, ducked underneath the crime scene tape, and motioned for us to get away from the scene. "Let's talk at the house."

We didn't argue with the detective as we quietly moved toward our sanctuary. Inside, we sat in the living room, huddled on the sofa. Detective Berry said, "This is tough news, but I wanted you to be the first to know. Cora was found deceased in the home. Obvious homicide, inflicted by Edison Gardenia. Edison exited the home with a gun raised and started shooting at my officers. They fired back. Edison is deceased. They're both dead. It's over."

A lot of emotions were swirling around in my mind and body. Disgust. Sadness. Anger. Love. Hope.

Ella and Ruby clutched one another. I placed my hand on Ella's back. "Are you two okay?"

They both nodded silently.

Grateful my family was safe, I still couldn't shake the thought that death was too good for Edison Carl Gardenia.

FORTY-ONE

Allison

THE DAYS, weeks, and months after Ella and Ruby were back in our lives seemed like a blur. There were a lot of things I hadn't even considered or thought of when we found them, like the press. It was quite a story. A girl gone missing twenty years ago found alive with a child from her captor. We learned there were representatives and lawyers to help combat those who wanted every detail of Ella and Ruby's story, and they became a big part of our lives for a while. It seemed like it was never ending.

Thankfully, after a few months back home, they gave us a bit of peace. Nearing midnight, on the day we found Ella and Ruby, once Mom arrived from the Bay Area, we made a family decision that Ella, Ruby, and I would move into Mom's house. Our family's home in the Bay Area. It wasn't a tough decision for any of us. We had spent too much time apart to live a two-hour plane ride away. It was much too far.

I sold the house, and by the grace of God — I learned God

was a big part of Ella and Ruby's life — I could keep my job at Troodle after a brief time off and relocation to the Mountain View office in the Bay Area. Even if I hadn't been able to keep the job, it wouldn't have affected my decision to move home.

But I was thankful, since the job gave me a distraction, as it always had. Mom, Ella, and Ruby had their own lives. I couldn't spend every single moment of mine trying to invade theirs. The reunification specialist who worked with Ella had warned us it would take her some time to get used to us and going out in public. Ella was used to being alone or with just Ruby.

We all had a lot of work to do. Ella and Ruby, and of course, me. A perpetual work-in-progress. I found a new therapist after explaining to Dr. Baker I thought it was best I see someone new. She didn't fight me and said that she was glad we found Ella and Ruby and wished me the best. After five years with Dr. Baker, I didn't miss her. But then again, I didn't miss those five years either. It was time for a new phase, and I liked my new therapist. She was smart and kind and we only met once a week in person. She didn't text me or send the police to my house, so that was a bonus.

Finding my sister didn't change the fact that I suffered from depression. It was a chemical imbalance that Dr. Baker and my new therapist, Dr. Gracen, explained I had likely been suffering with since my teen years. I had no more flashbacks and didn't attack any strangers thinking that they were Edison Carl Gardenia. The nightmares had mostly stopped, knowing the bad guys were gone forever and that my sister was finally safe and at home with us. I know, I know. I was nearing forty and still living at home. But I had spent too much time away from my family and wasn't in a hurry to get my own place. Although Mom and I had discussed it recently. She said that I wasn't getting any younger and I should try to date or find a partner because that was the normal thing to do. And hadn't I nearly perfected looking normal? Well, easier said than done.

My love life was pretty much nonexistent. But that didn't mean it would always be that way. Stranger things had happened. I mean, I found my sister after twenty years, when everybody else assumed she was gone, but in my heart I knew she wasn't. Was it divine intervention that led me to that neighborhood in Seattle? Or to that job at Troodle in the first place? I didn't know. I still didn't attend church and wasn't sure I believed in all of that. But something I couldn't explain had brought me there. Or it was all one big coincidence. Or fate. It didn't matter. Whatever it was, it brought us all back together.

Being home with everyone was different from what I expected. It wasn't like when Ella and I were growing up. For one, Dad was gone. And sometimes it hurt too much to think about how if he'd lived just six months longer, he would've seen Ella again. He would've known that she was okay. He would have met Ruby. But who knows? Maybe if all this God and heaven stuff is real, then Dad knows Ella is okay and is watching over his granddaughter.

I just wished they would have had one last hug, a kiss on the cheek, and that knowing smile they shared when they were conspiring against me during a board game. And oh, how he would've loved Ruby. I think he even would've taken a shine to Henry.

Henry, the man with a heart of gold. Whether he liked it or not, he was now one of our family members. Mom had invited him to weekly family dinners. He had, at first, agreed, albeit reluctantly. Initially he was shy and quiet at dinner, but over the last year, he'd opened up, and I referred to him as my brother, and Ruby called him Uncle Henry. Mom called him the son she'd always wished she had. I thought it was good for Henry. He even started dating a girl he met online and brought her to dinner. She was nice and shy but seemed to be quite enamored with Henry. We gave him the thumbs up and family seal of approval.

A year ago, everything seemed broken. My father had died. Mom was alone. I was alone in a strange city, narrowly avoiding the title of felon. It was like my life had been shattered. It just goes to show that you can't give up hope. Even when the day seems dark and there is no sunshine on the horizon, hope exists.

All I knew was I felt whole. It was like that piece of my heart that lay dormant had awakened. If I could summarize my current state of being, it was grateful. Grateful for my life and my family, both blood and chosen.

Ella

I pressed print on the computer screen and ran over to the printer, tapping the edges impatiently. *Just spit it out already!* It had been a crazy year but one that I knew would happen one day. I couldn't describe it, but I knew they'd find me. I prayed to God every day, sometimes twice a day, since I was grabbed and thrown into that van. I knew my fate wasn't with Edison and Cora forever. I knew one day Ruby and I would get out and find our way home. But at times, I still felt like a prisoner. Things were new and foreign. The press kept calling despite how long it had been. Publishers wanted me to write a book, a memoir of all the horrible things that happened to me. I told them I wasn't ready. Maybe I never would be.

My therapist said it would be good to write my thoughts and feelings in a journal and that it could be turned into a book later if I wanted. I wasn't sure that was the route I wanted to go. It might be healing for me, but I didn't know how Mom or Allison or Ruby would react to knowing exactly what happened to me. I didn't like thinking about it either. My therapist said that was avoidance, but I didn't really need to talk about it. I lived it. I survived it. I'm a survivor.

The printed paper caused a smile to spread across my face. After grabbing it from the tray, I ran down the hall into the dining room. Mom was fixing dinner, and Allison and Ruby hovered over the computer, as usual. The two engineers. Ruby had always reminded me of Allison, even when she was really tiny. Her analytical mind. Her love of all gadgets and computers, always wanting to know why things were the way they were. Always wanting to take things apart and put them back together again.

When Ruby told me they were going to let her attend public school and would be out in the world, I knew one day she would find Allison and bring us together. It's weird and silly and maybe I spent too much time praying to God while I was in that back yard.

I held up the paper. "I passed!"

Mom stopped stirring the sauce and ran over to hug me. "Congratulations. Well done, Ella."

"Thank you."

I don't think there were too many doubts that I would pass my GED exam, considering I was already looking at colleges for the fall. There were schools that offered hybrid classes where some were in person and some online, which would help with the social anxiety that I struggled with. But with the help of my therapist, it was getting better.

I had told Mom I wanted to help around the house and get a job. She told me I was silly and that my job was to be a student and a mother and that sometimes the order of things isn't how we plan, but it's what we have. She said she wanted to support me and give me everything she could. And she could support Ruby and me while I went to college. I was blessed.

But I wished Dad was here so he could meet Ruby. I

wished Edison, or 'Eddie' as he had me call him — gross — hadn't taken me, and I wished I hadn't gone through all that.

But there was a shiny silver lining. Ruby. She was my angel. If I hadn't had Ruby, I would've never survived. I would've lost hope. I would've given up, and I might've even taken my own life.

Ruby was doing so great. I don't think anybody questioned that except for her therapist, who didn't know Ruby very well. They encouraged her to go to school but warned all of us that Ruby may need a lot of help, but she didn't. I knew she wouldn't. Allison knew she wouldn't. Even Mom could see it. Ruby had immediately wanted to join the softball team and the robotics club. And within a week of starting school, she had two best friends, and the numbers grew every day. She was so outgoing and friendly, not hardened by our experience. And she'd already started nudging us to teach her how to drive. I'd only had my license for six months, so Mom and Allison agreed to help teach her. Even Henry offered.

Henry, what a guy. The brother we always wanted.

I still had nightmares, and I still worked through the days to try to forget the past and plan out my future. The next big thing would be college. I didn't quite know what I wanted to do for a career, but I had always loved art and music. Ruby suggested graphic design using computers. She insisted we could start a business together. She could be the techie, and I could be the creative. Like I said, she was my angel. I wasn't sure I wanted her stuck with me, but from what I could see, the world was ours for the taking. One step at a time.

THANK YOU!

Thank you for reading *The Neighbor Two Doors Down*. I hope you enjoyed reading it as much as I loved writing it. If you did, I would greatly appreciate if you could post a short review.

Reviews are crucial for any author and can make a huge difference in visibility of current and future works. Reviews allow us to continue doing what we love, *writing stories*. Not to mention, I would be forever grateful!

Thank you!

ALSO BY H.K. CHRISTIE

The Martina Monroe Series is a nail-biting crime thriller series starring PI Martina Monroe and her unofficial partner Detective August Hirsch of the Cold Case Squad. If you like high-stakes games, jaw-dropping twists, and suspense that will keep you on the edge of your seat, then you'll love the Martina Monroe crime thriller series.

The Selena Bailey Series (1 - 5) is a suspenseful series featuring a young Selena Bailey and her turbulent path to becoming a top notch kick-ass private investigator as led by her mentor, Martina Monroe.

A Permanent Mark A heartless killer. Weeks without answers. Can she move on when a murderer walks free? If you like riveting suspense and gripping mysteries then you'll love *A Permanent Mark* - starring a grown up Selena Bailey.

For a full catalog, or to purchase signed paperbacks and audiobooks direct from H.K. Christie go to: www.authorhkchristie.com

At www.authorhkchristie.com you can also sign up for the H.K. Christie reader club where you'll be the first to hear about upcoming novels, new releases, giveaways, promotions, and a **free e-copy of the prequel to the Martina Monroe Thriller Series, *Crashing Down*!**

JOIN H.K. CHRISTIE'S READER CLUB

Join my reader club to be the first to hear about upcoming novels, new releases, giveaways, promotions, as well as, a **free e-copy** of the **prequel to the Martina Monroe thriller series**, *Crashing Down.*

It's completely free to sign up and you'll never be spammed by me, you can opt out easily at any time.

Sign up today at
www.authorhkchristie.com

ABOUT THE AUTHOR

H. K. Christie watched horror films far too early in life. Inspired by the likes of Dean Koontz, true crime podcasts, and a vivid imagination she now writes suspenseful thrillers where justice and hope prevail. *The Neighbor Two Doors Down* is her eighteenth book.

When not working on her latest novel, she can be found eating & drinking with friends, walking around the lakes, or playing with her favorite furry pal, Charles T. Snickerdoodle.

She is a native and current resident of the San Francisco Bay Area.

www.authorhkchristie.com

ACKNOWLEDGMENTS

This story came to me after reading Jaycee Dugard's first memoir, *A Stolen Life*, a memoir. If you don't know her story, Jaycee was kidnapped in 1991 when she was only eleven years old. She was then held captive for eighteen years living in the backyard of a couple in the San Francisco Bay Area. During that time she was repeatedly assaulted and gave birth to two children. She was discovered, alive with her two children, in 2009 when her abductor's parole officer grew suspicious of some his activities. The case is horrific, but also a symbol of Jaycee and her daughter's strength to endure what they had gone through.

I only recently read the memoir but the story has haunted me since Jaycee was discovered being held captive *less than a mile* from my sister's house. I had driven past the home Jaycee was held in *for years*, while she had been imprisoned there. It still sends a shiver down my spine. Talk about a monster in your own neighborhood.

Jaycee and her daughter's seem to be thriving, according to her memoir, and that fills my heart with hope. This goes to show you that although Allison and Ella's story is a complete work of fiction, it isn't implausible. There is always hope.

I want to extend my deepest gratitude to my beta readers and my advanced reader team. My ARC Team is invaluable in taking the first look at my stories and spreading awareness of my stories through their reviews and kind words. To my editor

Paula Lester, a huge thank you for your careful edits and helpful comments. And many thanks to my proof reader, Becky Stewart. To my cover designer, Odile, thank you for your guidance and talent. To my husband and my dog, Charlie, thank you for supporting me in every thing I do.

Last but not least, thank you for reading my books. It's most appreciated. Without you I couldn't continue doing what I love - writing stories.

Printed in the USA
CPSIA information can be obtained
at www.ICGtesting.com
LVHW042357170124
769269LV00036B/1038